THE HISTORY OF THE BAKER'S DOZEN

GARY FINCKE

The History of the Baker's Dozen by Gary Fincke
978-1-949790-94-8   Paperback
978-1-949790-95-5   Ebook

Cover art: Shannon Fincke
Layout and book design by Mark Givens
First Pelekinesis Printing 2024
For information:
Pelekinesis
112 Harvard Ave #65
Claremont, CA 91711 USA

Library of Congress Cataloging-in-Publication Data

Names: Fincke, Gary, author.
Title: The history of the baker's dozen / Gary Fincke.
Identifiers: LCCN 2024014904 (print) | LCCN 2024014905 (ebook) | ISBN
    9781949790948 (paperback) | ISBN 9781949790955 (ebook)
Subjects: LCGFT: Short stories.
Classification: LCC PS3556.I457 H58 2024 (print) | LCC PS3556.I457
    (ebook) | DDC 813/.54--dc23/eng/20240403
LC record available at https://lccn.loc.gov/2024014904
LC ebook record available at https://lccn.loc.gov/2024014905

www.pelekinesis.com

The History of the Baker's Dozen

Gary Fincke

CONTENTS

I

10   *Albatross*
12   *The History of the Baker's Dozen*
14   *Extant*
18   *Beauty*
20   *Teaching English in the Biology Lab*
21   *The Plagues in Order*
23   *After the Death of Sons*
26   *Where Boys Waited for his Daughter*
27   *Standing around the Hearts*
29   *Elevations*
32   *How My Mother Posed Me*
33   *Tapeworm: A Parable*
35   *Marking the Solstice*
37   *Sideshow*
41   *Tractors*
44   *After Hospice, the Uses for Liquor*
46   *The Hands*
47   *During the Plague Years*
49   *Inflatables*
52   *Little Pricks*
55   *Shadowing the Gravedigger*
58   *Shopping for the Future*
61   *The Bedroom Clowns*
63   *I Married a Monster from Outer Space*
66   *The Drive-Thru Peep Show*
69   *Ash Wednesday*
71   *The Year of Spooling Backward*
73   *The Bottled Ghosts*
75   *Prom Weekend*
78   *After January's Active Shooter Drill*

80   *The Guest-Closet Ball*
83   *While he Still Drives his Father's Car*
85   *Happy Endings*
88   *Hansel*

II

92   *Boxing the Future*
110   *The Times*

III

128   *Stunned*
129   *Wail*
131   *Summiting*
134   *The Look-Alike Doll*
135   *IQ Test*
138   *Kafkaesque*
140   *The Au Pair*
144   *The Year of Extravagant Additions*
147   *After Six Years, the News*
151   *Lazarus in the Forest*
153   *Among the Swings*
155   *Apocalypse*
158   *The Pre-Need Obituary*
160   *Angel Number*
163   *I'm Doing the Talking*
165   *Writing Letters for the Blind*
168   *Quagmire*
171   *Metaphors*
174   *What Trouble Meant*
176   *The Theory of Dog Shit*
178   *Translating the Hawk*
181   *Surrogates*
184   *Zipper*
187   *Aeration*
189   *Negligees*

192   *The Devil's Children*
194   *Postcards*
197   *Christmas Sweater*
201   *Headlights*
203   *Years Later, the Once-Famous Mailed Girl Tells her Story*
205   *Lessons*
208   *What Color Did*
210   *Holidays*
213   *Friday was Condors and Whooping Cranes*

I

ALBATROSS

After twenty-five years and an hour of cash bar drinks, the ballroom-sized venue is stuffed with chatter and assessment. From classmate to classmate, you listen to the stories fat with nostalgia or self-regard, all of them rooted in achievement. You nod and smile and sometimes spew your own stories, pleased by the attention. Your wife, who graduated a thousand miles from here, has slimmed down for the evening. As if she is here to discover your past, she listens more closely than you to what your classmates say. She follows your eyes from woman to woman.

More than an hour, it takes, for the classmate you dreamed about in biology, chemistry, and physics to reach you. After graduation, all summer at the pool, she was a lifeguard, but you only imagined her in a swimsuit because you worked a union factory job. Also, if you were honest, because you couldn't swim. Regardless, your wife is comparing her to the yearbook photos you have shown her more than once.

You feel sixteen again, nearly afraid, but she talks as if you were more than a dreamer, plunging into her story about another boy who could not swim. Hand-over-hand, she says, that boy must have edged to deep water along the dock that claimed part of a lake for the summer camp where she worked after college. No matter the reason, he'd lost his grip and gone under while she'd scolded another boy for running, adding a minute between her whistles for buddy checks. "Last warning," she quotes herself saying to the running boy. "Don't let me see that again."

For twenty-two years now, she says, her dreams often have soundtracks of whistles and screams. Always, there is wa-ter-with-shadow, a still life. She wakes with what feels like a heavy weight yoked over her arms. Twice each night, she rises to check the breathing of her four children who sleep paired in two rooms. A trilling in her ears insists that she evaluate the pillows, examine the chests for the temporary relief of rise and fall.

You don't mention a word about how, though you still can't swim, you have practiced CPR on a dummy called Mike Muscles, bringing him back from the dead with your hands and breath because you coach something as landlocked as a tennis team. "Imagine yourself watching a boy dragged from a swimming pool," the class instructor had told you. "Imagine your well-trained hands on his chest is the only way to resur-rect him."

Now, you don't say a word at all, but you notice she is look-ing at your name tag, her mouth forming and then reforming the three difficult syllables of your last name. As she begins to turn away, your wife says, "Michael and I are both so sorry."

The woman lays one hand on your wife's arm. "Safety is impossible," she says, her voice hushed as if speaking only to your wife. "There's no shame in the inability to comfort."

The History of the Baker's Dozen

Though he has never short-weighted his bread, the baker knows there are rumors. Air is deceptive, the baked size inexact, but for cookies, cupcakes, doughnuts and sweet rolls, he gives thirteen to the dozen, all those extras insurance against accusations of fraud.

As it's always been, that gesture is popular, but lately, there's been grumbling about size, how his sweets are shrinking like candy bars or boxes of sugared cereal. Counting on the power of transparent numbers, he offers fourteen to the dozen. It's a fool's count, an out-of-business sacrifice, but his reputation flowers, customers buying in multiples of dozens, gorging themselves on sweet rolls until they begin to grow fat, suspicious about his loss-leaders, sure that the generous numbers for his baker's dozen must be hiding something.

When the baker, anxious now, stuffs fifteen sugar-rich items in a box, smearing the icing or scattering the powdered sugar, the conspiracy theories multiply. Everyone sees that he is the thinnest man in town. That his size means he avoids his extras. A boycott is called for. His silhouette is a synonym for what the heavy hate.

When he tries sixteen for the price of twelve, the boycott cracks and crumbles. The customers smile and gorge themselves. They lick their fingers, reaching for seconds and thirds, but it's not long before they bad-mouth him again. Stomachs oozing over their belts like unwatched dough, they curse and call him names. "Thief," they shout. "Robber," they scream as they carry their overstuffed boxes away. They refuse to buy his bread. They threaten him online.

When, at last, the baker doubles the dozen, not raising the price, graffiti flourishes on more than the bakery walls. Nothing could account for "Buy one get one free" but fraud. Demonstrations are called for. When out-of-town reporters arrive, the customers protest *en masse* outside the bakery, holding up signs saying CHEAT and EVIL printed on flattened, grease-stained boxes.

The night that the bakery burns, every customer says that they knew it was only a matter of time until that skinny baker destroyed what used to be a place like paradise. Thirteen had raised suspicion for centuries, but adding to it was proof that corruption prospered among the ovens, cheating secretly stored in the bins and sacks and refrigerators. What's more, absolutely, without a doubt, and forever certain, nothing but unpardonable sins could be for free.

Extant

It was my wife's idea to stay at a stranger's house for the holiday weekend, sleeping in a room just down the hall from them for two nights and eating two breakfasts they cooked for us. Even worse was having them clear the table while offering us more coffee and hovering a few moments to coax compliments for a meal no one has ever seen on a diner's breakfast menu. Not the best way, I thought, for my wife and I to start over after being separated for nearly a year.

As it turned out, after we didn't do anything for New Year's Eve but go to a matinee and eat dinner at a neighborhood restaurant, there was an opportunity, at nine o'clock, for our hosts to offer a tour of the house. My wife was eager. There wasn't a way for me to say "No," not without a television in our room and none in sight in the living room.

Once we started in the kitchen with the island large enough to seat four in the middle, the husband excused himself to brush snow flurries from the sidewalks. We were barely into the living room when the wife said, "There used to be a stripper pole here." She pointed so vaguely that I pictured the pole in several places. The living room was large enough for a dozen poles. When she paused as if silence held that information in the air, I added a stripper to that history, her nearly naked body gripping the pole with her thighs.

"Who lived here then?" my wife said.

"Two pornographers," the woman said at once. "They filmed here. There's a movie about them. The Porn Barons. Maybe you've seen it on Hulu? A documentary. This room, the whole house for that matter, looks different in the film."

I started imagining those differences, but the woman, after my wife and I both shook our heads, went on. "They made a fortune, but they ended up in jail. They fought about money and one of them was killed there before their sentences ended. The surviving porn baron is dead, too, natural causes."

Upstairs, two of the four bedrooms were as large as most living rooms. The phrase "on location" seemed to seep from their walls. From our unobstructed view, the property was perfectly landscaped all the way to the edge of the half-frozen, natural lake. The woman explained that they had remodeled the house for the second time eight years ago. That the change followed only three years after the one they'd had done before they moved in. As if the house needed to be disinfected, I thought, and then, shortly thereafter, they'd discovered an even deeper cleaning was necessary.

The master bedroom sported an enormous flat-screen. The room sprawled so much larger than ours that it comfortably housed an oversized bed, one that could easily support a threesome or perhaps an orgy. The drapes looked so thick that nothing could ever be seen by prowlers. Outside, the world was frigid. The wind, when we'd returned from the restaurant, had been blowing gusts of twenty, even thirty miles per hour, but when she stopped speaking, allowing us to gape, the room was soundless, as if secrets of any kind could be kept.

The husband was waiting when we came back downstairs. "The pole she told you about was right here where I'm standing," he said at once. "Long gone, but those old movies are still extant."

My wife smiled like she does when she is making a deci=
sion, but I was trying to form a sentence with "extant" some=
where inside it and all I heard was an echo. Those actors, if
they were veterans, would have been at ease in the house, the
stripper pole an early prop or a feature used at launch par=
ties, maybe even stylized into a logo. Decorated somehow.
Sparkling. Reminding audiences of the excitement of earli=
er films, promising more of the same, but with a freshening
twist. For sure, the house was large enough to handle dozens
of variations.

At ten-thirty, we shared an early champagne toast with our
hosts before slipping between what my wife pointed out were
very expensive sheets. "I'll stay up," she said. "Just to read."

I stayed awake doing nothing but wishing to sleep, but she
nudged me at five minutes to midnight. "Get dressed," she
said, not asking. She led me through a door to the room's ex=
clusive balcony. The air was still now, but I was shivering in
just the jacket I'd thrown over pajamas. My wife was better
prepared in hat and scarf and gloves. "It's just a minute now,"
she said. "It's been years since this."

I clutched myself and concentrated on *this*. Our hosts, both
armed now, appeared on a next=door balcony and fired the
first of six shots each into the air, the reports, though seconds
apart, so close to simultaneous that they must have rehearsed.
"She told me," my wife said, after I kissed her quickly and
headed inside. "She offered a rifle, but I said we'd at least be
outside to watch."

The next morning's meal was called brunch. We were at the
table for more than an hour, the food so elaborate and served
so late that lunch was out of the question. We had hours to
fill before another movie and dinner.

When we returned to our room, the bed was made. Not a surprise, except we both saw right away that the bedspread was different. "Weird," I said, but it was my wife who noticed that the painting over the bed had been changed as well. "Wow," I said, and she held that smile of hers for a few seconds.

At last, she said, "It's like a movie location."

"Like we've been gone a while," I said.

"Yes," she said, her hands sliding up under my untucked shirt. "Like something's changed. Like something different is about to happen."

BEAUTY

When Shelly gets to college, she learns that money is as necessary as her half of a room and pre-paid cafeteria meals. That most of her classmates used money like air and water. Repeatedly. Without thinking. Expecting the same from everyone else, including her.

Sure, there was menial work available—in the cafeteria, with a maintenance crew, or, a bit better, as a clerk in the library or a department office. But at minimum wage, Shelly shelved books and updated magazines for three months without changing anything, two weeks wages spent in one day.

She heard about the escorts scattered among older students. She didn't have the body, she thought. Or the face. Or the indecency. But she remembered how often her feet were praised. How, when she wore sandals, someone would say, "You're so cute down there with your painted toe nails and smooth skin."

She could model, a job that had potential. An entrepreneur now, she made a portfolio. She submitted her feet. For a week, she expected agencies to contact her. Or Etsy sellers who needed promotion. Shoe companies. Podiatry websites. Some site besides the ones popular with creeps.

For another month, she waited. She used that time to investigate. If only the weird would pay for her feet, she needed to be sure they never found her. Anonymous wasn't a perk. Sure, the site charged a 20% fee on all her sales, but it didn't require an ID, something, even protected, impossible to perfectly secure, even with an anonymous email and only digital payments.

She trimmed her toenails. She practiced poses. The varieties of color and design. Glitter. The ways to seduce and please. How much to charge. If she resisted additional exposure, she was selling such a small part of herself that it wasn't like selling at all, no different than cleaning up after the rich and careless.

Soles were desired. Close ups. Spread toes were admired. Arches sexy, curves created when she stood on her toes. Or her feet in heels, one sleek shoe dangling near jewelry, flowers or lit candles set along a marble floor.

Her mother had always said "Show your best side." There were men who hungered for exactly that. They paid to dream, leaving her untouched and unknown. She would never tell on herself, not this beauty she'd become, the best part of her adored.

Teaching English in the Biology Lab

Sea life charts are props for Melville, the mounted cat a visual aid for Poe. Leaves are displayed like a nod to Thoreau.

Biology is frogs dissected, worms halved and pinned, the lesson of finding life in mouth scrapings. Those sophomores are looking at the muscles of pigs with awe. They are learning the networks of nerves where pleasure and pain begin.

When the first new reckless driver dies, the fetuses swim in jars as if they might still be born. The skull atop the desk waits as if I can throw my voice, as if it's about to speak.

THE PLAGUES IN ORDER

For Children's Day, the primary Sunday School classes put on a play about Exodus. The third graders had speaking parts—Moses, the Pharaoh, an assortment of Israelites and Egyptians. The minister stood in the darkened choir loft to speak the words of God each time Moses needed to hear them. The first and second graders were the plagues in order.

Under two red bed spreads, the second graders were a river turned to blood. Masked and hopping, the five first graders were frogs before the second graders were lice and then flies. Finished jumping, the boy could hear the murmurs of the adults from the shadowed pews.

Part of a herd of cattle, he went on all fours and lowed like the teacher had taught them. The Pharaoh hardened his heart again while the five of them milled around in black and white outfits until they buckled and fell onto their sides because God had killed them.

The second graders wore white hoods circled by the red of boils Everybody flung brown rice as hail before they all chattered like locusts. Finally, like the others, he put on a black sheet and waited for every light but the one at the base of the chancel to go out before they walked around slowly. The church seemed to spin as he and six other boys dropped and died, the rest of his classmates stepping back and back until only he, like the other first-borns were lying in the dark. When half the lights switched back on, the boy lay still while the Israelites walked between two pieces of plywood painted to look like waves.

That night his family talked about the plagues, what they would be if they were trying to get out of Pittsburgh. "A flood, for sure," his father said. "Heavy snow followed by rain and a sudden thaw."

"The Atom-bomb," his mother said, and his grandmother shook her head and made the tsk sound with her tongue she always used when she was displeased.

"The first-born would get polio," his aunt said. "They'd have to live in iron lungs."

"Tsk," the boy's grandmother said. His aunt looked at him and said, "Not you, Bobby. You're not first-born if you're the only one."

His grandmother cleared her throat. "Smallpox," she said, and the boy smiled, rolling up his sleeve to show off the mark on his shoulder.

"I'm safe," he said. "All of us are safe." He'd seen the scars on his parents. His mother's mark was twice the size of his, as big as a quarter.

His grandmother began to lift the hem of her dress, and suddenly, on the outside of her thigh, a scar the size of a silver dollar appeared. It was milky and concave, not like anyone else's. "A plague on the fool who gave me this," she said as it shimmered. She pulled her dress back down.

That white circle seemed to shine through the cloth. "Leukemia," he said, remembering his cousin Greg.

"The first-born," his aunt said.

"That's enough for one night," his grandmother said. "That's enough about the plagues." For then, it was. For six years until his mother brought a dark diagnosis home, a word no one had spoken that night, a plague nobody in the family had ever heard of.

After the Death of Sons

In a museum dedicated to man-made landscapes, a virtual elevator lowers one couple through Earth's calibrated crust, temperature rising from coal mine to gold mine to deepest bore hole, heats verified until they are safely in hell. Neither says a word about how terrible some deep and overheated jobs could be. Neither mentions how they were once taught the threat of eternal flames as if that lesson was essential as mastering cursive writing. What they both know is the elevator has not descended as deeply as "the death of sons."

After those sudden deaths, some of that couple's acquaintances and friends chorused in-person condolences. Some called to try commiseration buffered by distance. Some texted their twice-removed sympathy. Some settled upon signing an attendance sheet of public tribute. All, by now, have been embarrassed to silence by helplessness, their well-wishing changing every one of those days as little as prayer, their language unable to form an alibi for God or the school bus driver losing control.

One son, eleven, had been fascinated by the intricacy of knots; the other, twelve, had loved the strokes of swimming's medley relay. One bedroom wall displays bowline and square, sheepshank, clove hitch, and tripod lashing, all those twisted cords arranged under glass like monarchs. The opposite wall photo-celebrates Michael Phelps X 4, the recent hero of butterfly, breast, back, and free.

Because the father listens to nothing else but the music of rage, his body sometimes clenches and stiffens, his blood thickening in his throat until he hurls and thrusts the closest object, whether book, chair, dish, or cue stick. Because he is often empty-handed, he settles for his fists, weapons he uses on his basement wall, refusing, afterwards, to mask the breakage, claiming that those scars are comforting, surrogates for the damage he dreams upon that driver.

Because the mother once listened to someone explain mindfulness, she keeps the silence of ghosts. Because that moderator, at last, asked her to write her thoughts in columns headed *To be done. Maybe later. To delete.* Because that mentor said, "Send those that are erasable into space to create the rapture for your distractions," she refurbishes that year-old page like a failed mall, filling it with *never.*

Sometimes, a counselor tells them, a second language is necessary for what we suffer, the longing for impossible just beyond the borders of English. She offers *Tesknota*, 'the pain of distance" in Polish, a longing, beyond nostalgia, for more than the past. Sometimes, the counselor does not speak because she is afraid she is about to lie.

Often, the father dreams of family, his wife a frequent character, the voice of their daughter, nine, from the doorway after midnight, her questions progressing, phrase by phrase, from anxiety to dread to fear. His wife approaches like a survivor emerging from catastrophe, their street always behind her, its devastation obscured by swirling fog or smoke.

Often, the mother sees their sons in their former room, searching for things they hid when young, toy cars and tiny, coded, secret notes wedged in where they expected them to survive, untouched, forever. Both boys sleep as late as vampires. They return at night like livestock.

Always, late at night and still downstairs, the couple's conversations end in limbo. Always, when they rise from their chairs at last, they approach each other with so much sorrow in their arms that they cannot lift them to embrace. Always, their daughter cries and calls. Always, their sons are silent overheard, even as they move from room to room.

WHERE BOYS WAITED FOR HIS DAUGHTER

Just inside the front door, standing mute and still and looking anywhere but his face.

On the porch, like a delivery boy, like what he was carrying was light but awkward.

In his driveway, inside a car, the window rolled down, the motor running, speaker bass vibrating.

Across the street, shadowed until he cupped his hands to light a cigarette

A block away, the car radio muted, headlights extinguished

Outside of town, in a public park she drove to in his car

In a dorm room at the local college

Inside an apartment walking distance from campus.

Wherever lurking was possible, where they decided, if she was alone, whether to act or only imagine; whether they were boys who took risks; whether they were boys who had waited long enough for what they wanted.

Standing Around the Hearts

In first period health class, all twenty of us stood around the cow's heart Miss Hutchings unwrapped on her desk. "Inside and out," she said, "we need to know ourselves," halving that heart with a scalpel to show us auricles, ventricles, valves, and the wall well-built or else. Her fingers declared where arteries begin. She pressed the ends of veins.

Richard Turner, whose father's heart had halted, examined his hands. Anne Cole, whose father had revived to cut hair at the mall, stared at the floor, ducking the entry to the steer's aorta, the four chambers we were required to know.

While we watched, Miss Hutchings, who knew nothing of our families, unwrapped the refrigerated hearts of chickens and turkeys, swine and sheep. She arranged them by size on the thick, brown butcher paper, leaving a space, we knew, for ours. Frank Kratzer, who was excused from gym, drifted behind us.

Miss Hutchings, who sometimes forgot our names, had us take our pulses. We listened to each other by way of her stethoscopes, boy to boy, girl to girl, because of the chance we would touch. Those chilled hearts warmed while I dreamed of pressing my ear to the rhythmic heart of Stephanie Romig, whose breasts, so far, had brushed me one time while dancing.

And then Miss Hutchings said, "You have ten pints of blood inside you, sometimes more or less, depending on your size. Whoever is largest almost surely has the most," and Alma Booker snapped the lead of the school pencil she used, like all of us, for taking notes. Miss Hutchings didn't pause. She said, "Your hearts, so far, have beat half a billion times. On average, they will beat two more billion times," leaving us to calculate our futures while Frank Kratzer backed through the open door and vanished.

He didn't hear what Miss Hutchings said as she gathered the hearts to return them to ice. How the blood has so many routes to follow, their total would take us around the world and back. How our capillaries are so close to the surface, that where the skin is thinnest, like on our lips, it is the most sensitive. All of us were paying attention when Miss Hutchings said, "Think of how a kiss is a pleasure," but then she paused, cradling the cow's heart, and all of us, no matter our size and shape, seemed to bow our heads, secretly thinking of how our blood, even for the unhappiest, rushed to the sensitive sources for joy.

ELEVATIONS

My boy, thirty-two this week and still aimless, said he's bringing his girlfriend to visit for his birthday. Not the first time, but the other one visited from three blocks away for his senior prom, which maybe doesn't count, you decide. She's forty-eight, he says, like I might be interested in mulling that over, but she looks his age when they walk in, like she's been in one of the cryogenic pods space travelers use for trips to faraway galaxies. So, I'm thinking maybe this will work out, her mothering him, his body looking middle-aged since he dropped out of college with nothing to show for the two years except forty pounds of not-so-attractive flesh.

But wait, before you start thinking you've heard this one before, let me tell you about her disability. That's what she called it, "my disability," like she'd bought a puppy at the animal shelter to save it, and now it's a full-grown nuisance. She said she has a thing with elevation changes. I nodded. My ears have popped in descending planes and on highways ascending into the Rockies. But no, hers is nothing like common.

She's been living at 1,000 feet, she said. Like she's measured it. Like she searched for a place perched on a round number. The problem is we're at 1,217 here in Pennsylvania, which is causing her discomfort that's testing her pain threshold. Never mind what you're already considering—the drive here, the ups and downs.

And hiking? Not mountain climbing, mind you. Hiking anywhere but Kansas. She's sensitive to differences of more than fifteen feet, she says—up or down—so hiking near where I live is pretty much out except around the yard. The stairs, thank God, only take her eight and a half feet up or down, but we use three floors here. She calculated the risk and chose the bedrooms, which are upstairs, saying she could do without the entertainment in the basement for now. And she was cheery about it, saying it the way some folks tell a story about a wedding, say. Or the way she interrupted herself to reminisce about when, during her barista shift, she spied my boy in Starbucks, noticing how he sat in the corner where the only two cushioned chairs are located. No hardbacks for him. She deduced that right off, him being there for an hour mid-morning after the rush, that other cushioned chair an invitation.

She made a hard stop to look at what I took for a Fit-Bit, maybe a special one that kept an eye on the elevation while it counted calories burned from walking in circles. My son, the gentleman, let her have her silence for a minute (I started counting the seconds). Then she snapped back into focus and announced that the Starbucks she was talking about sits at 1,006 feet, and it's just two streets from her first-floor apartment, an arrangement, now that my son was part of it, made in heaven.

Like you might expect by now, there was more. The coma. The six years she was under its spell, the length of it maybe explaining her looking younger than you'd expect. A pint-sized, female Rip Van Winkle who said, three times that first hour she was under my roof, she came out of it no worse for wear.

Well, I should stop right there because some might be offended. I get it. That woman has had some tough breaks, a few more, for sure, than my son the Tik-Tok addict, and now they have each other and are happy. Or so it seems, him honoring her elevation thing by letting her lead, him taking the long way here, adding ninety miles to what is normally a two-hour trip in order to make their approach as gradual as possible. What he confessed had been an enormous, meandering set of pseudo-switchbacks, a lot of back roads and even a few U-turns, trying a different, less-steep road, including one not exactly paved and with three one-lane bridges.

Their trip made for story-telling. It kept me listening on the front porch that stands only two steps up and down, well within her comfort zone, something she demonstrated a few times, walking down and then up, smiling all the while, showing her boyfriend's mother that things could work out just fine. That they knew the best way here now and could visit often, snaking uphill in loops and circles that added only an extra two hours, maybe not even, now that the roads were familiar, to the trip. The roads, my son showed me, were highlighted in that old atlas he'd taken with him a decade ago, its pages all marked up by my husband before he passed because he was always in charge of finding our way to wherever and back. That artifact was getting a new life, a few pages already with hand-drawn red routes snaking across the chunks of two states the two of them had figured out how to travel, a necessity, they both agreed, now that they were desperately in love.

HOW MY MOTHER POSED ME

The photographer instructs my mother to hide under the dark maroon blanket to hold her infant still. "It takes time and quiet for your darling to be perfect," he says. In all of his portraits, she sees that nothing disguises the shape of the mothers, the way the cloth narrows at their heads, the taut geometry of their laps. Regardless, she lets him cover her and cradles my body through cotton. Loose threads stroke her face. She sweats throughout the lengthy shot, laboring in the darkness to aid the wonder of permanence, holding her breath to become inanimate for love.

Tapeworm: A Parable

After he says that her latest diet has failed. After a morning of cajoling and an afternoon of his sweetest talk. After her reluctance at twilight, he tells her, "This one is foolproof." After darkness sets in, her resistance wavering ever so slightly, he says, "Never again will you need a new one."

After he swears this will be the greatest gift he could give her. After she travels with him to Mexico on what he calls a "working vacation." After she accepts the nausea that surrounds her and jabbers in her ears while she swallows the advertised meal of infected beef. After this diet, at last, has entered her, he kisses her, but not, she notices, upon the lips.

When they are about to leave, no one has to warn, "Say nothing to anyone." When she sees another well-dressed couple pass them, she is grateful for dark glasses. When they step outside, she adjusts her wide-brimmed hat, tugging it ever-so-slightly lower.

Now, the heat and swirling dust announce what feels to her like cartel weather. Already, she imagines the guaranteed worm devouring her. She remembers health class, the filthy boy in front of her who sucked his fat fingers after his greasy lunch. Aftertaste flies home with her. "The future," it promises, "is two pounds lost per week while you eat the food you love."

He reminds her that trust is what's necessary. That a miscarried worm is the exception. When her body thins and lightens, envy will examine her full plates. Jealousy will notice that she doesn't excuse herself from the table. Rage may even drum its fingers or clench its fists throughout the unshakable alibis of dessert, after dinner drinks, and more than an hour of conversation.

"For certain," he says, "the worm will keep its secret. What better arrangement could it wish for, regularly fed and undisturbed?"

She wonders how many weeks it will take for him to be pleased. How many, after that, until he worships her. She has nothing to do, now, but wait.

So, there is time for her to study. To learn that the segments of her worm are conjoined to absorb her through their skin, that it will fatten and lengthen from its greed for her without relying upon an insistent mouth.

For two months, he does nothing but watch her, saying that he is waiting for perfection. For another month, the same, promising and promising like an evangelist. When she is dizzy, he says, "Trust." When she is nauseous, he says, "Faith." She begins to dream him thin and frail and gasping. She studies cleansing.

Because she cannot announce by using bottled remedies, she learns that flushing the worm requires papaya seeds in warm water and honey. She hydrates and repeats until one promise, at last, comes true. For three days, her weight is steady. On the fourth morning, she has edged up three ounces. He hovers over her lunch. He stares at her dinner. The following morning, she begins to leave him, pound by pound.

Marking the Solstice

Because I was born on my mother's birthday, our parties were divided into day and night. My friends, full of cake and ice cream, left before dinner. My mother's friends arrived at twilight, drinking wine as the mid-summer sky went dark. But each year, at noon, before either party began, she asked me into the yard to wait for the moment she said the sun would pause before its annual slow decline.

Our birthday was June 21st, and I was eight before I learned that the solstice didn't happen on that day every year. Because I loved seeing her so happy, I never told her I knew which years we were late, that the sun had changed directions the day before. I loved that impossible story she told while we waited for twelve o'clock and the tolling of the bell from the church three blocks away. "It's as far north as it ever gets," she would say, "and now it begins to scuttle backwards, like our astral sign, toward winter."

The summer before I started high school, the solstice was June 20th--Gemini, not Cancer--but she called me, as she always did, a few minutes before noon. By then, I'd learned, that her body, like the sun, was already crawling backward toward ice. What would kill her had begun in her arms and legs, medicines that might slow, but could not ever cure, in the purse that clung to her each time she left the house. What I also knew, by then, was that crabs, nearly always, walk sideways, not backwards. That if you thought about that the right way, it meant they stayed in the same place, not coming or going.

That June, standing near the living room picture window, she paused for a moment to show me two old towels that had been wedding presents, ones worn so thin by fifteen years of use that the sunlight filtered through them. She handed me one and kept the other for herself. "Nothing is gone," she said, "if you keep it." She led me to the dining room clock she wound daily and asked me to turn the key. On our way through the kitchen, she pointed out the old rotary phone and said it was as good as new. Outside, we walked past the ancient station wagon she said would last until I would learn to drive on it, mastering the stick shift that the world was forgetting.

Then, in the yard, noon about to arrive in the year that would mark the middle of my time with her, she handed me the key to the three rooms she rented for us until I was seven. "You'll thank me someday," she said as the church bell began counting to twelve. "And keep this one, too," she said, handing me a thin, but heavy key I'd never seen before, the one, she explained, to where she had lived with my father for a year without me. Where those towels we were holding hung thick and bright. Where, after an evening shower, she often wrapped her body inside one for warmth as she walked to the bedroom to part the wedding-present sheets and unlocked herself, welcoming the possibility of me into this world.

SIDESHOW

The summer I was about to turn fourteen my sister, just out of high school, class of '62, went headless. "We're perfectly spaced," she'd said since she'd started ninth grade. "When you're ready for high school, I'll be gone."

She'd met a guy during the winter. "A carnie," she said, "Ok?" the third time I asked. "But he's a handyman during offseason." After I let it slip to our father at dinner, she told him, "I know what you're thinking, but they're not all bad people."

Dad looked grim. He kept his eyes on Susan while she glared at me and said that the carnie, whose name was Ronnie Czak, had got her hired as Justina, the headless girl. "All I have to do is sit there," she said. "I'm supposed to have been decapitated in a car crash and saved by a doctor who knows how to keep my body alive while he's waiting for a head to attach."

"It's not your head I'm worried about," Dad said.

Two days later, Dad was looking out the window at a man standing beside a powder blue Impala that was creased along the passenger side as if it had sideswiped an iron fist. "A man parks at the far end of the driveway and doesn't come to the door isn't a good thing," he said.

Susan was holding a small duffel bag that was sized for an overnight trip, but she'd already tossed a big suitcase into the back seat of the Impala. Dad was holding a drink like he always did after work. "It's just a job," Susan said. "It's people shopping. It's no different than standing behind a counter in a department store."

For a moment, when our father moved away from the window, he looked like a man who would stand in the doorway and take my sister's fists and feet until she exhausted herself and gave up. "Who do you think you are?" he said, but he stood so far from the door she could walk around him at more than arm's length. When she opened the door, he didn't turn. "You think you're all grown up now?" he said, but he was facing me and his voice trembled.

My sister left the door open so Dad, for a few seconds, must have thought she was hesitating. "Think about it," he said, his voice sounding more confident. His hands tugged at his shirt as if he were smoothing it before he turned to confront her. He took three deep breaths before I said, "She's gone, Dad."

His hands fluttered back to his shirt and then dropped to his side. "Close the door then," he said. "The house will be full of flies."

I didn't move. With the door open, the light in the room seemed to shimmer as if we were near water. The sound of tires on gravel churned into the house and then spun away. I walked to my room. A minute passed before I heard the front door shut and the sound of the bolt sliding into place. I heard the refrigerator open and ice cubes dropping into a glass.

Susan called once a week, always mid-morning when Dad was at work. "I'm fine," she said, and then she listened to me say how boring summer was. Dad never mentioned her until late July when he called in sick on a Friday and told me to get dressed and get in the car because we were going sightseeing.

The carnival, an hour from our house, was set up in the parking lot of a big discount store that had closed a few years before, the lines for the spaces visible as we walked toward the entrance. "Your mother is lucky she's dead" was the only thing Dad said when we saw the sign—**Justina! Kept Alive through the Miracle of Science.**

He didn't say another word, but he handed over two quarters, and we slipped inside. Sure enough, where Justina's head should have been were tubes arching up from between her shoulders, a thick one in the middle like a fat artery and eight more curling off it like spider's legs.

Ronnie Czak hovered over her, fiddling with one of the tubes as if Justina might be in distress. He was dressed as if he'd just stepped out of an operating room. Light blue scrubs, a surgical mask dangling below his chin, thin transparent gloves on his hands. Justina had been rushed to a hospital, bleeding badly, a recorded voice told us. She'd been given transfusions. A famous doctor knew how to keep her body alive while a search went on for a new head to replace Justina's disfigured, brain-damaged one. It had been months now, and yet here she was, the doctor still hoping.

Dad stared at Ronnie, but I was focused on Justina's outfit, a halter top that showed cleavage and a skirt that didn't reach her knees. Without a head, Justina looked like a girl I'd think about until I had to lock the bathroom door and stroke. A few murmurs rolled up when Justina moved her hand. "She's not a dummy," someone said. "She's real." I glanced at Dad to see how he was taking it, but now he was looking at the other customers, maybe a dozen of them standing around and gawking, all of them men.

When we left the trailer, my father walked up to the pitch man. "That Justina you have sitting in there," Dad said. "She's my daughter." I thought of Dad examining Justina's body to be sure she was Susan, what parts of her made him certain, but the pitch man nodded as if a headless girl was easy to identify. "You keep that to yourself and I'll pass it along."

My father seemed satisfied. He bought us French fries and we waited. "You'll never see a headless boy at the carnival," he said. "You're old enough to get my drift. Am I right?"

"Right," I said, but Susan was already walking toward us wearing shorts and a white blouse buttoned almost to her throat. For a moment, she sized up Dad's expression. "Hi Dad," she said. "I'm ok. See?" Dad looked past her as if he expected to see Ronnie, but she was alone and nobody else noticed her. Nobody knew she was Justina, who maybe they'd paid to see. All she had to do was change clothes and give everyone a look at her face, something that made me feel as old as my father. Someone sad, as if I was alone way before I ever expected to be.

TRACTORS

Once, in May, a tractor near where the teacher lived in Western New York vanished beneath the earth when a farmer drove too early into the onion fields. The teacher, a month from finishing his first year of instructing teenagers, drove twenty miles to stare at what he had read was a John Deere, large and green, as it rose from the mud, heaved up by pulleys. Someone in the crowd that was watching said that the farmer, as his tractor sank, had stood, riding until his shoes had touched the soil. Someone standing near the teacher laughed. "A temporary Jesus, that fool was," he said, "believing he wouldn't drown that tractor."

One of the teacher's home room students, fifteen that spring, had lost an eye in a farm accident several years earlier. The empty socket had been stitched closed. Her hair always hung across the nearby scars like a veil. None of the other teachers knew whether or not she would receive an artificial eye or plastic surgery, but the teacher heard stories. The one he heard most often claimed the girl was piggyback riding her father like a model for the joy of family farming. The detail included each time said the girl had been wearing shorts and a t-shirt because the early May weather, that year, had been warm, the soil supporting the weight of the tractor. Only once did someone, a colleague in the faculty lounge, say that the father's black Harvester tractor had flushed birds and turned over two nests of mice before it bucked and tossed the girl. The teacher didn't ask how that woman could possibly know that.

That summer, the younger brother of one of the teacher's students, tumbled under the harrow that trailed what the newspaper described as his father's red New Holland. Before the service, the boy who had been in one of the teacher's English classes looked at the floor, not speaking, when the teacher reached his spot in the receiving line. The father sat beside the minister in a pew apart from the family. During the funeral, the minister said, "Remember the eight years of joy that child has brought," as if, the teacher thought, the dead boy had been that farmer's pet. After the service, the father rushed from the church, his shoulders so hunched it appeared as if he was being dragged.

In September, the girl with one eye was in the teacher's first-period class. For a month, her head always tilted down toward her opened book, she never answered when he called on her. In October, he asked her to read aloud a story's important paragraph. When she began at once, the class listened closely. Several hands went up before the teacher even asked a question. Each week, as fall drifted into winter, she flawlessly read what he asked for. Always, the teacher's first question brought an outburst of raised hands.

In March, the boy whose brother had been killed quit school. In May, before she began reading, the girl, without looking up, said she loved the story's unhappy ending because everyone kept secrets about themselves that deserved punishment. Instead of the passage that the teacher had asked for, she read the last page, her voice tuned so perfectly to the despair of the characters that no one spoke when she finished, even when the teacher did not ask a question until the girl, after several seconds went by, looked up, her hair parting to expose her damaged eye.

The teacher, after school, silenced his car radio and drove into the country, choosing back roads with little traffic. He drove slowly, as if he was looking for an unmarked address. He rolled his window down as he passed a field where a tractor was being driven. He listened closely as he passed two more busy tractors. At last, he turned onto a rutted, gravel road, slowing further. He passed an expanse of what would become onion fields before he saw a deep-blue tractor. Though it was a dozen rows deep in the level field, it stood still. The teacher could not identify its make, but he could clearly see that the farmer was crouched beside it. Not as if he were examining it. The teacher could hear that the tractor was smoothly idling. Moreover, the farmer faced away from the tractor, his eyes fixed on the plowed earth between the road and where he crouched. As if he was lost in thought. As if, like the teacher, he felt ghost-like, and was waiting to re-enter his body.

After Hospice, the Uses for Liquor

Housecleaning, the new widow finds the box of partially filled liquor bottles her husband had moved from Colorado, keeping them to use only when the friends he'd shared them with came to visit in Delaware. "Those friends only," he'd said. "No exceptions," but no one, for thirty years, had visited from Colorado, the carefully packed box forgotten. Could all those liquors still be good? For nearly forty years, she'd sipped her social drinks only when she'd needed to. When her husband had asked. When he was entertaining clients. When drinks were investments, as useful as the mementoes she'd boxed and brought from Colorado—her father's tools, her mother's coffee pot and cookbooks and baking tins.

What they'd always agreed upon--preservation was important, waste unacceptable. And now that these bottles needed a use to find them, she began to empty them, starting with easy recipes, making Preserved Figs by letting them marinate in sweet brandy. By using the gin for a bowl of what one of her cookbooks called Maple Macerated Berries, infusing them with a mixture of salt, lime juice, and what was left in that bottle. And then she began to bake. She measured a portion of the bourbon for Brown Sugar Pound Cake, brushing a syrup infused with it over the top, sampling small slices for weeks. She added a part of the vodka to the dough for a cherry-almond pie. She finished the bourbon by preparing Honey Peach Preserves, what the cookbook claimed was a match made in heaven when fresh thyme tied everything together. She concocted vanilla ice cream into Brennan's Banana Foster, burning off the sauce made from butter, brown sugar, cinnamon, and the Colorado rum.

The hospice had been "long-term," a paradox she had embraced and then dreaded. She did not make Steak Diane, her husband's restaurant favorite, refusing all of the red-meat recipes, but she prepared shrimp vodka pasta, pork with mango and rum sauce, and tequila-glazed chicken thighs. At last, as the anniversary of her husband's death approached, all of the bottles but one were empty. She set them on the windowsills of her bedroom where they caught the late afternoon light in shades of green and blue and something suggestively pink that she rearranged so that it would deepen before the others. Satisfied, she began to make fruit cakes, six of them, as many as she had the Colorado cognac for. Using one of her husband's shot glasses, she divided that cognac into one-and-one-half-ounce portions. Slowly and carefully, she poured them over the fruitcakes, pleased when barely any ran off. The tins were already lined with plastic wrap. Because she had emptied an entire shelf, there was room for all six in the refrigerator. She knew that fruitcake lasted and lasted. That night, she dated each tin. She could still be eating them a year from now, maybe more. A few small slices might outlive her. Though they had never had children, her brother had four, more than enough to take care of things after her death. One of them would find the last, partially-eaten cake, notice the date, and be filled with wonder the way small, ancient artifacts preserved in glaciers or peat bogs strike awe in their discoverers, this dessert she had baked gone on for something like forever.

The Hands

In magazines and newspapers, my great uncle, for decades, was a hand model. He used lotions and creams, my mother said. Regularly. Frequently. According to my father, those hands looked as if they had never done a day's work, even in age, smooth, white, untouched. My father's hands were always white with flour, dusted to roll dough into spheres, left and right handed, to model forms for sandwich buns while I relied upon the right, unable, after seven years of Friday night work, to master the art of left-handed circles. Years before, bare-handed, a man had pulled a pan of sandwich buns from the oven without burning his hands. My father, some Fridays, would tell that story whenever miracles were mentioned. As if we needed faith while that man never again forgot his gloves. As if we needed to believe a woman born with three fingers experienced, after amputation, a phantom hand with five fingers. As if those bones had needed years of weather to expose them. Now, my daughter, an artist, teaches anatomy to small children, beginning, each year, with the hands. Miraculously, her daughter, at five, drew my hands like a camera. My mother had a small scrapbook of clipped ads that featured hands. Here, she said, are your uncle's, and there, too. Looking was like taking an IQ test. Which of these are identical? Which one of those doesn't belong? My mother's uncle lived forty years beyond modeling, his hands so unspotted for so long they seemed to suggest that his body was unspeakably pink and soft.

DURING THE PLAGUE YEARS

For his appointments, two years and counting, the woman who cut his hair was always masked when she unlocked the door and recorded his temperature like a dedicated nurse. Every eight weeks, she opened early on Thursdays to accommodate his fear, the salon empty, her partner not due for half an hour, his hair self-washed just minutes before. Her mask was always leopard-spot print, his black. The radio was flush with current pop songs. With what he often felt was tenderness, she lifted the loops of his mask from his ears to trim.

Years before, like his daughter, she had failed algebra, the two of them miserable, but together in summer school. For six weeks, they had been friends, a coincidence that made conversation easy. "Solve for x," she said. "Solve for y," and they laughed about no longer remembering which function came first to perform among addition, subtraction, multiplication, or division.

But then, in late spring, the third year begun, she said, "It's been crazy" before murmuring the details of how her former husband had been shot and killed while outdoor-eating chicken wings, the gun, moreover, home-made by the jealous shooter. He did not interrupt her. Most of all, he did not admit that he had no idea the dead man had been her husband. That he knew her only by her high school name, the one brought home by his daughter more than twenty years before.

She touched up his goatee and clipped his unruly eyebrows. She confessed that though her ex had been with a woman who was also dead, the first to be shot, she had been sleepless since. After she brushed his loose hair to the floor, she showed him a photograph of her two teenage daughters, their father no longer absent, but gone. "This daughter," she said, "drives her dead father's car to work and washes it by hand each week. That daughter wears his shirts to bed." As she allowed him a moment with the hand-held mirror, he remembered simultaneous equations, how, years ago, they were a way to solve for three unknowns, something he kept to himself like a terrible perversion.

At last, she said she was thinking she could live without cutting and styling hair. His spoken sympathy, he knew, did not comfort her. He paid in cash, his tip, a habit now, pre-calculated to minimize the chance of contact. Already, he was telling himself never to speak of this to anyone, and yet, weeks before she vanished and his hair was cut by a young, beautiful stranger, he betrayed her.

Inflatables

"Enough about Santa Claus," our father said last Thanksgiving. "His visits are so far apart, you start thinking he's never coming back. St. Bernard's are heavyweights. They're faithful. They're rescue dogs for a reason."

As if that explained the enormous, inflatable St. Bernard. Enormous an understatement, gigantic closer, the balloon as wide as half the yard we'd once played in with a dog named Champion that weighed, full-grown, fourteen pounds. "Champion," our father had said way more than once, "is a bantamweight." My brother and I had no idea what the St. Bernard's fighting weight was, but its paws stretched from the property line on one side to the middle of the yard where a brick walk led to the front door.

Our father said he hadn't named his new pet, but King Kong came to mind because the dog was so tall it looked right into the front bedrooms on the second floor. Not quite Macy's Parade size, but larger than any inflatable in the town where my brother and I had grown up watching our parents decorating the house and yard during the Thanksgiving weekend as if Santa in New York City meant Christmas could come early to small-town, central Pennsylvania.

Our father, who still worked the garden center at Lowe's and wintered there in large appliances, didn't touch our house when we were boys. "That's your mother's business," he'd say, and every year she surrounded the front door with a single strand of alternating, tasteful blue and white lights.

Meanwhile, our father always attacked the yard with strings

of red and orange and yellow, a narrow spectrum of what he took for heat, ignoring that the hottest flames were white and blue. He slathered the hedge that covered the exposed cinderblock across the front of the house. The yard was too small to support much more than a weeping cherry on one side of the walk, but he wove a web through its branches and lit it. Gloriously garish. A signifier. "Wildfire," he'd say. Our mother said "brothel" until we were old enough to understand.

As if that made him reconsider, he put out that fire and had us help him inflate a fat Santa whose sleigh sported a propeller that swirled. As it grew dark, we noticed that Santa's body lit up from the inside. From then on, our father beamed, each Thanksgiving, until, four years ago, the weeping cherry tree died and so did our mother.

After that, just those blue and whites remained, the lights in place year-round. Santa, deflated, stayed stored among an assortment of seldom-used tools in the backyard shed. "I'm trying," he would say as we ate the turkey dinner he'd picked up from the grocery. Three years of that, but then, both of us pushing thirty and giving financial independence a tentative try in Virginia and Ohio, we made the trip back and found that St. Bernard already staked out and inflated when we arrived, Santa a flat, wrinkly mess at the bottom of a small dumpster our father said he'd rented to contain the results of "a good, old-fashioned house-cleaning."

A sign of recovery, my brother and I agreed, but now, we have returned for Easter, and the St. Bernard is still inflated, half the yard nearly smothered by a balloon as if only children lived here. "There's been complaints," our father admits, both of us nodding because the dumpster is still in the driveway. He catches our look and waves us closer to the dog, nearly underneath its belly. "The kids from the elementary school love it. They call it Superdog. The kids from the intermediate school call it Giganticus."

"What do the middle school kids call it?" my brother says, glancing up, so much innuendo in his voice that I interrupt.

"There's probably an ordinance about this, Dad," I say. "There will be fines."

"Or somebody," my brother says, "will just stab it in a dozen places."

"It would take a cold, cold heart to do that," our father says.

"Or no heart whatsoever," I say, and my brother nods, accepting the hint.

Our father brightens. "I'm doing the ham myself tomorrow."

It's late March, Easter come early this year, and when it begins to rain, our father opens the front door and calls us over. Surrounded by the blue and white lights, we watch the St. Bernard glisten and sway, the leftover gray snow turning to slush. "Your mother loved dogs," he says, and ushers us back inside.

Soon, there's enough wind to angle that rain against the house in a modestly noisy pelt, and when my brother and I are upstairs in our old twin beds, that St. Bernard's large, round eyes drift side to side outside the window. Our father hasn't unplugged the dog, and its big head is still illuminated from the inside in a way that makes us agree his expression looks concerned, even soulful, the face of a savior.

LITTLE PRICKS

"Check this out," Ted Ball said. "They go ape-shit over their nuts and bolts in here," and you checked the aisles to see who might go ape-shit in the hardware store at the version of the Miracle Mile closest to your house. You didn't see anybody except two grandfathers and a bored clerk as Ted picked up a wrench and looked around like an apprentice thief. His twin brother Thad handled screwdrivers and pulled his coat together; he fondled a power drill and jammed both hands deep into the trench coat's pockets. "Come on," Ted said, and, sure enough, as soon as all of you cleared the front door, you heard "Boys" from behind. The twins kept walking, so you kept pace. There were two other possible targets on the sidewalk. And then *Roy Sellers, Store Manager,* according to his red tag, stepped in front of you and demanded that you open your coats and turn out your pockets right there on the sidewalk of the shopping center in front of the anchor store, a crowd blooming around you like dandelions.

"Not you," Roy Sellers said when you unbuttoned your pea coat, but the twins were so slow with their pockets he kept saying, "The coats. Open the coats." And then Ted and Thad peeled down their zippers and spread those coats, turning circles so everyone could see they had nothing to hide. "You little pricks," Roy Sellers said. "You goddamn bastards."

The twins laughed about it while you hiked the mile back to their street. "You little prick," Ted said, shoving Thad. "You goddamn bastard."

When you threw rocks at stray cats with the Ball twins,

you hurled your stone when they did, trying to make sure they didn't notice your rock always missed. To keep your secret, you cheered like they did when one of the stones made the cat squeak and run. They always quit after that, the cat quickly gone. "Boring," Ted would say. "Same old, same old," Thad would agree. "Yeah," you said each time. The Ball twins lived across the street. There weren't any other boys your age within half a mile. You watched them, one Saturday, set out tuna from a can, something to hold any cat's attention while they got close enough for Thad to spray it with lighter fluid while Ted dropped a lit match.

The cat seemed to expand and then it ran a few steps and rolled, extinguishing flames which leapt back as soon as it turned. "Nice," Ted said, but already, as you backed up, he seemed far away. By the time the cat stopped rolling, the fire spotty across its body, you'd doubled the distance, so intently watching the last of the flames go out that the twins could have come at you from either side with the rest of the lighter fluid and an open flame. "You little prick," Thad said to Ted. "You goddamned bastard." They didn't say anything to you because you had already crossed the street.

"Nobody lives in that direction," Ted said, pointing, one afternoon when their parents were gone for the day, toward the vacant lot that ended where the woods began. "We can shoot anything over there."

Thad was excited. "Squirrels," he said. "They're almost tame around here." Ted had the .22 in his hands, bringing it up to his shoulder while the nearest squirrel busied itself among the acorns near a stand of oaks. "Your turn is next," Thad said to you, moving up on Ted's right to get a better look.

You clapped his hands together, the squirrel skittered, and Ted half-turned, his finger still on the trigger. "Damn it," he started, and then the gun went off and Thad grabbed at his leg above the knee, and went down. "Oh Christ," Ted said. "Oh Jesus. Now what?"

You held your breath and released it slowly, something your junior high track coach had told you to do as you settled into your starting blocks. You watched Thad's jeans darken; you saw how pale he was. *Get hold of yourself*, you thought, but you couldn't, even as your father ran by, pulling off his belt as he knelt, tying it around Thad's thigh, knotting it and then lifting Thad to carry him to the blue station wagon as Ted followed.

The doors slammed and they were gone, but you could still hear Thad wheezing as he went by, small dry coughs exploding from his open mouth. You wanted to tell somebody. To explain. But there was nobody bursting from any other nearby house to ask what you were doing there when a rifle fired. Instead, you had time to form an answer: Just watching, mostly fascinated, almost innocent, not some little prick who needed a lesson even though now you'd had one.

SHADOWING THE GRAVEDIGGER

Because the gravedigger agreed when Jack asked to ride with him, Jack is in his truck waiting for a mid-winter funeral to finish. "I keep my distance," the gravedigger says. He shifts his body to expose more of his window, leans back as if he expects Jack, a student at the nearby university, to calculate the yards between them and the gathering by the grave. To show respect, Jack is wearing a topcoat instead of a hooded sweatshirt. It nearly covers his jeans.

The funeral is in blue and white, the team colors of the same university where Jack is a senior. There are enlarged photographs of football teams, all of them too distant for faces, names or years. At the end of the just-completed season, the university's team had suffered a devastating bowl game loss. Jack's father had watched the game on television. Twice, during the game, he'd called to tell Jack the score. "It's a close one," he'd said both times, leaving that message on Jack's voice mail.

The windows fog the funeral away, and the gravedigger does not rub his side window or any part of the windshield clear. He says, "You never want to park too close, so you learn how far away is necessary to be discrete." He taps the dashboard. "And for damn sure," he adds, "never play the radio."

When Jack asks about the difficulty of his work in winter, the gravedigger falls into storytelling. He says there are times he has shoveled by hand for infants and the cremated, holes too small for the oversized spade of machinery. For those, weather is important; the earth, if frozen, is a bitch. The funeral, by now, is invisible. When the gravedigger goes quiet, Jack looks straight ahead, breathes a small cloud, and remembers.

Below zero, it was, the day his mother was buried, backhoe visible on a nearby rise, mound of earth covered by something designed to look like summer sod. The minister labored at turning January into meaning, snow and zero entwined until everyone at the gravesite chorused the chilled amen of erasure. His father had stood by himself at a distance. Like a visitor. By the time Jack and his mother's sister had thanked the minister for being willing to hold part of the brief service outside despite the cold, his father was gone.

Out loud, but nearly whispering, Jack tells the gravedigger he has watched, recently, as an urn was laid into a grave behind a local church. The girl was a suicide. The mother a neighbor, the father in another state. Their one surviving daughter, the same age as Jack, shoveled soil while the minister recited a prayer everyone could follow by reading a printed program. When he reached the bottom of the page, Jack felt like shrieking. The minister invited everyone to a covered-dish lunch. Jack sat with a small plate of untouched food as if an uneaten sandwich could stand in for a phrase of sympathy.

The gravedigger nods and wipes his side window clear. The small crowd has begun their retreat to roadside cars. A woman is carrying the oversized photographs. Two men have easels in their arms. "A child must be the most difficult," Jack tries, and the gravedigger says that he's opened and closed the earth for his father, that now his mother has entered hospice. Jack muffles the remainder of his experiences until they are smothered.

"Whatever you can bear," the gravedigger says, and he opens his door, the weather rushing inside the truck, reminding Jack to follow.

Shopping for the Future

"Your mother's pregnant again," my father told my sister and me. "A surprise," he added, like the news was part of a riddle. My sister was nine; I was nearly eleven. What we were doing, my father had just explained, was shopping for the future, browsing the options. For half an hour, we'd been following a salesman out into the country, a place so deserted, I thought he had had taken a wrong turn. But now, though the world still looked empty, we had arrived.

The houses, it turned out, were bunkers nearly buried in the ground. The agent, after we stood in front of one, mentioned Hiroshima and Nagasaki, Kennedy and Kruschev and Cuba. "What?" my sister whispered to me. "Who?" but I shook my head like she wasn't supposed to ask.

"Next time," the agent said. "things will be worse, the bombs more widespread and deadly, but this home you're inspecting was built by the government with just that in mind. It's guaranteed to withstand an atomic blast."

My mother spoke up. "That's enough about that," she said, and pointed at my sister and me. It was early summer, but she tugged her coat tight against her body.

"Ok," the agent said. "Just remember, the future will take you hostage. On that, you can count." My mother glanced longingly at where our car was parked nearby. She took my sister's hand and my father stiffened as the realtor boosted his voice a notch. "Most folks," he said, "and maybe the both of you, are more concerned about natural disasters like the pandemic. Things are starting to happen—supply chains crumbling, tens of millions out of work—something, for sure, is coming our way." Then he looked directly at my mother and said, "Rest assured, this area is connected by one hundred miles of private roads."

All I could see was an empty plain stretched out in every direction from where we were standing. All over the nearest land, in what looked like straight rows and columns, steel doors were tucked into identical grassy humps that gave away the locations of the bunkers. "A house should be a sanctuary," the realtor said as we followed him inside one to take a look. "This one has room enough for as many as ten, more comfortable, of course, with fewer."

No matter how roomy that bunker was, even my father had issues at once, reasons for hesitation and doubt. When he pointed out that the interior seemed like a shell, the realtor admitted that electricity, plumbing, and properly filtered air were what he dubbed "necessary extras."

My father frowned. My mother said, "We're through here." The realtor didn't seem discouraged. He reminded my parents of how little one of those bunkers cost. "Around $40,000," he exclaimed. "About the same as a single-wide and a million times safer." He thumped the ceiling to remind them that what they were buying was the life insurance of being firmly underground. "There is another site a thousand miles east of here," he said, "but most people prefer the added value of remote, far north, distant from floods, hurricanes, tornadoes, and military targets. Once everything is installed, you'll appreciate the absolute accuracy of the phrase 'location, location, location.'"

My parents listened a little longer. They discussed the difficulties of what they called "downsizing," something, my father said, "was as necessary as potable water."

"Every purchaser shares your concerns about having too much to carry, the tough choices they need to make," the realtor said. When neither of my parents immediately answered, he smiled brightly and said, "It won't be nearly as hard as Noah had it."

Outside again, the realtor made one more push. "Look how the mounds are arranged so geometrically. From far above, if lit, they would look like a postmodern constellation."

My parents weren't swayed by what my fifth grade teacher had called "figurative language," but when they admitted they were interested, but still unsure, the realtor became excited. "There are more reasons to buy than I've mentioned."

When my mother said, "What else might convince us?" he smiled and lowered his voice.

"Once you're inside, you need protection from those who are outside. The have-nots are going to go after the haves. They will knock on your door. They will be desperate. They will get ugly. But you'll have apocalypse-protection." He paused, flinging one arm back toward the heavy, relocked door. "Or, if you prefer, think of it this way: Your family's safety is what you'll have in common with the high net worth families who spend millions elsewhere on their bunkers."

All of us stood there among the bunkers, the wind blowing steadily across the treeless plain. The realtor watched my parents, evaluating. When my mother let go of my sister's hand, I knew that she was going to say "yes." That she recognized we needed to move. "After the baby is born," my father said, as if there was one more border to cross, as if we were refugees.

THE BEDROOM CLOWNS

Without asking him, the boy's mother has his room redecorated. The clown wallpaper fills two walls after his mother drives him home from school, the cars and motorcycles that seemed to drive right at him when he entered the room or lay in bed vanished. "Everybody loves clowns," she says. "It was time for a change, and the man who hung it was happy for the work."

The boy decides that all of the clowns on his new wallpaper are falling. He stares, counting and recounting how often each of the clowns is repeated. Three clowns are brilliant in solid colors—yellow, red, and orange. As if dressed in school colors, four are two-toned. Three are in stripes whose spirals make them appear to spin. All of their suits are baggy, each of them uselessly ballooned, their enormous shoes spread like helpless sails.

Just barely, the boy shudders, but his mother is worrying about his silence. "Don't they all look happy?" she says. The clowns' expressions are painted sunny and gleeful, but each one, the boy notices, wears the same white foundation of deletion.

"They look silly," he finally says.

"Good," his mother says, relieved. "That's their job."

The evening passes without the boy returning the grins of the ten clowns. What he begins to believe is that those that are splayed sideways are scudding across what appears to be a cloudless, wind-swept sky. That some who seem to be seated on nothing are plummeting from an unseen plane. Worse are the twisted, head-first clowns, their bright smiles lasting all the way to the carpet where their legs still pedal air as he feels the floor fall out from under him.

Worst of all, he thinks before sleep, are the arms-extended clowns who are grinning as they concentrate on maintaining impossible flight. From behind them, inside the wall, the boy hears the scratching that accompanies their disguised fright.

In the morning, like she has since the accident, his mother drives him to school using a road that adds two miles to the trip. "The scenic road," she calls it, as if the scenery had begun to matter now that he was in second grade. The boy, as he does each day, silently promises to ride his new bike on the old road as soon as he dares to disobey his mother's "Sidewalks only."

That afternoon, nearly finished with the scenic road home, the boy asks his mother about sky, where it begins. At the far edge of everything, she tells him. Like heaven. Where clear weather is always expected and no one you love ever leaves. The clowns, then, must fall from above the sun, he decides, but all day he has been thinking that they are being carried up by a violent wind.

When he returns to his room, he closes the door and presses the lock. The clowns are still tumbling, but the boy, this time, believes they are ascending, their half-seen bodies near the ceiling proof. When, standing in his father's floppy shoes, he holds his smile exactly like theirs, he feels he might lift and rise if he doesn't cry. That he would learn where his father has gone if he, too, could vanish.

I Married a Monster from Outer Space

On Friday nights, after my father left without a forwarding address when I was twelve, my mother and I watched old horror movies together. Double features. I picked one. She picked one. There were plenty of them out there, but for the first few months I chose nothing but the ones where insects and oddly shaped animals blew up into giants. Spiders and ants. A praying mantis. Crabs and an octopus. And once, even a pack of rabbits. My mother said, "Oh wow" and "Cool" and "What will they think of next?" but I could tell she paid more attention to the ones she selected, mostly mad scientists trying to raise the dead or merciless aliens invading Earth.

"Take your time, Gerry," she said one Friday night. I was scrolling through the site that gave one-paragraph summaries of horror movies, each one decorated by an original, old poster. "Find one that's really special, one that might be your favorite since the night we started."

So I looked a second time, bored, even then, by all the Godzilla lookalikes and King Kong rip-offs. I knew my mother would be disappointed if I chose anything that even my ancient Sunday School teacher would recognize. Finally, I fixed on one—"Attack of the Giant Leeches"—*A depraved, bloodsucking, sinister force*, according to the poster. "That's a good one, Gerry," my mother said. "Any sized leech is disgusting."

The movie was terrible, mostly because the leeches didn't look real when it came time for them to do some bloodsucking. My mother made popcorn between features. She plopped down on the couch, passed me the bowl, and said, "Watch closely, Gerry. This one I've seen before. This one is perfect."

The title was "I Married a Monster from Outer Space," but the woman in the movie was already married, only now, an alien had kidnapped her man and stolen his body. It was an easy switch, the way it always seemed to be for the crea- tures who arrived in spaceships. But now, that woman had to wonder why her husband was so distant. "Look at that cold, handsome fish," my mother said. "She has to know what's up with that."

That husband, I could tell, had a problem. He had to go home day after day to the horror of something ugly that wanted to be touched, something that couldn't leave him alone, all for the sake of having that body bear his children. The woman was worried. Then sad. Then angry. No matter her sexy lingerie, nothing about her seemed to be getting through to her husband.

But then, with maybe fifteen minutes still to go, my mother shut the movie off. "That's it for the perfect part," she said. "The rest is the same old children's story. I bet you know what I mean, Gerry. The ending that never happens."

For sure, I knew what she meant. Already, I was sick of acting like I was big and all grown up. Those ants and spi- ders get slaughtered no matter how huge they get. Even the rabbits, despite their size, are destroyed by people who are mostly stupid and afraid until one of them gets lucky, com- ing up with a way to save the world in a way anybody watch- ing would have thought of before the movie was halfway fin- ished. That alien my mother had chosen was smarter than that woman's husband. How else would he be able to fly so far? And that happy ending, the real husband returning and the alien defeated? I knew that was impossible. That woman was stuck no matter who opened the bedroom door, the indifferent alien or the fool that had been replaced with no one else that she knew, the wiser.

THE DRIVE-THRU PEEP SHOW

Twice a week, Frank goes early, paying to watch when the window opens. Usually, he is first to arrive. If not, the line is never more than two cars, something that's happened only once during the sixteen months Frank's been a regular. Like having a tee time for privacy, he thinks, making sure things happen on schedule. Since the pandemic, he works from home, but nothing has changed about his diligence. There is always time, before nine, for entertainment and need.

His wife is a teacher, gone each day by 7:30. The booth opens at 8, and Frank lives only nine miles away from the drive-in, close enough to make it by 8, far enough to lessen the chances of his car being identified. Better yet, the booth the woman uses is a discreet distance from the highway. If there is another such drive-thru in the entire state, he has never heard of it. Where the woman works her magic reminds him of a turnpike toll booth, another thing that has almost disappeared, something he secretly misses, always, whether leaving after one exit or dozens, prepared with the exact change.

But this morning, his car seems to cough as it idles beside the opening window. It sputters and stalls. Minutes later, when he tries to restart it, the engine refuses to turn over. The window, by now, is closed again, the woman, one of three he has watched during the long pandemic months, is shuttered. He hopes, even prays a little, that the threatening weather will keep customers away, but that wishful thinking is soon smothered by a car pulling in behind him. When that driver notices the window isn't open, he taps his horn.

Frank tries the engine again. Nothing. Now, the horn tap is an extended bleat, its insistence stripping Frank until he feels as naked as that woman becomes just as her performance ends. Half-dressed again, she must be listening, alert, maybe nervous, imagining that the horn is a policeman's method of asking her to step outside.

He thinks of paying a second time, that maybe all that his car engine needs is a few more minutes to recuperate. Instead, realistic, he hunches down, prepared not to show his face if that driver approaches on foot. He could be a neighbor. A friend. Even his younger brother, who lives only twelve miles away in the opposite direction.

He spends thirty seconds in that bomb-drill position, the car horn, like an air-raid siren, finding a rhythm of its own. Head down, he calls AAA. When the dispatcher asks for his location, he says, "A couple of hundred yards past the red light on Route 22."

"Which light?" the dispatcher says. "The one right before Climax?"

"I think so," Frank says, and the dispatcher, thankfully, laughs and says, "Gotcha, buddy." It's his lucky day, the dispatcher goes on, an available truck very soon on its way to his location.

Only nine minutes, the AAA mechanic takes to arrive. Even better, that anxious driver behind him has backed up and driven away. It's only 8:36; Frank guesses he can still check in on time if it's just a quick jump start. Already, he is forming his vow to have the battery checked. Something like promising the dentist that he'll floss daily. An analogy he will share with the man who will rescue him, someone who might joke with him about being caught with his pants down.

But when the truck door opens, the driver who steps out is a woman. As she walks toward him, she asks for his AAA ID, the card he has already tugged from his wallet, the one with his name clearly shown above the long, launch code number that hasn't changed in the decades he's carried the annually updated one with him. The one, he discovers, she expects to receive from him in open space beside the car's left headlight.

She is expressionless as she inspects his car. The battery is fully charged, she says, the problem somewhere else. She spews something about the carburetor, and after Frank only nods, his head bowed, she points it out to him as if she is certain he knows nothing about the anatomy of a motor. When she says she will tow it to the garage of his choice, Frank, for a moment, believes she is asking for his address.

She raps on the closed peep-show window and says, "Sorry, in there. Engine trouble out here."

Two fresh cars turn into the long driveway. They are so close together, Frank thinks they are unmarked police cars. The AAA driver watches them for only a second before she turns to face Frank. "Need a lift?" she says, but Frank's tongue has gone spongy and slack.

Ash Wednesday

Despite the snow, his mother insists that the neighborhood is feverish, running a temperature raised by the nearby mill. Their house keeps gathering a film of filth, jaundiced by the industrial air. The city bus drops the disappointed off at the end of the street. Because sidewalks live somewhere else, plows a total stranger, they follow the furrows left in the snow by tires, open doors, and disappear.

Like his birthday, Lent has returned, its Wednesday evenings, non-negotiable, sentenced to sermons and communion and lost television. Earlier today, the next-door Catholic girl was spotted with ashes by a priest, her forehead a neglected windowsill. Last summer, thirteen, he watched her body tan on the other side of the hedge of hollyhocks. From his upstairs window, the pane so small it could be called a keyhole, he stared and stared and memorized. All winter she has entered and exited the cars of junior and senior boys.

Now, after he asks about ashes to pause her on the shoveled sidewalk, she explains how her thoughts are synonyms for sins both venial and mortal. "Yours, too," she says, and though he has not been taught to distinguish, he knows that he has practiced gluttony for years and laughed about it. That he lies and swears and sometimes, though petty, he steals, all of those sins so common to his friends that they must be venial or else heaven is empty.

Later, while his mother's minister starts his annual interpretation of Lent's stories, he remembers that spot of ash, certain his deepest secret is a mortal sin. Not his daily waking to lust, but his all-day watching only the channel devoted to it, his body mortgaged to obedience, unable to pay down that debt. How, right now, he wishes to be a priest who overhears the mortal sins, listening and listening for one of the guilty and sorrowful to explicitly confess what is thrilling enough to damn him.

The Year of Spooling Backward

Like my school, the year began in late August when my father's older brother, the World War II veteran, buys the first extended-family movie camera. On Labor Day, we learn to wave when we visit the pond he makes us call a lake. After he squints into the camera, he tells us our first movie lesson is to do something besides standing still in our swimsuits. Moving when we're photographed takes some getting used to, and our smiles, at first, are stuck at grimace on his warped dock. At last, my twelve-year-old cousin simply jumps, legs bent, nose held, and thrashes, yelling for me and my aunt to follow his leap into the algae-covered pond/lake.

In that first film, we finish with waves from the waist-deep water, then vanish, my uncle's camera swinging up to where the crippled elm displays what would be its last summer of leaves. For a few seconds, the home movie ascends higher into an explosion of sun that seems to burn the reel to darkness. That's all there is, but when my uncle shows it on a bare, dining room wall, it doesn't end there. The sun pauses before the elm hovers and each of us leaps back to the dock, feet under us, suits dry, hands dropping to our sides as we marvel, in the dining room, at our hilarious, mannequin selves.

In November, the day we get our first report cards, Mr. Wentz rewinds the mushroom cloud produced by an A-bomb test, shrinking success down into its bullet-shaped shell. A platoon of soldiers rises from where their uniformed bodies had lain prone in freshly-dug trenches near ground zero.

They lift off their dark glasses before backpedaling into a sea of light that fills with words that multiply into lists and paragraphs. When I tell my uncle about my fifth-grade teacher's movie, he says, "That man needs his head examined. You can't rewind the bomb."

In January, thrown from his Buick ice-spun into an oncoming truck, my uncle dies. For three days, a row of photographs flashbacks him from father to soldier to groom. A second row takes him to teenager to a boy my age to a baby held by my grandfather, who is wearing his uniform from World War I. Sixteen other relatives arrive, but during the funeral, only my aunt and cousin sit beside my grandfather, who seems so shrunken in a high-backed chair he looks smaller than either of them.

Just before the service begins, my father, who missed the war because he was deaf in one ear, fixes my blue clip-on tie and buttons the too-small sport coat handed down two years before from my cousin, who is wearing a tight-fitting dark gray blazer I know I'll be wearing soon, maybe even for Memorial Day, when all of those relatives, like always, will come back to have dinner together, the adults talking about wars while my cousins and I celebrate the end of school as if we all believe it will never begin again.

THE BOTTLED GHOSTS

Late in the afternoon, the auction nearly over, the bottled ghosts are offered for sale. Two of them, each in its own tightly sealed jar. The room divides into laughter and silent attention. One is an old man, the auctioneer explains. The other a young girl.

When bidding begins, the old man is offered first. Tentatively, paddles are raised for his glass-encased ghost. The bidding, though, is lukewarm. Every gesture is scrutinized by a dozen smirking faces. The successful bidder, however, believes his purchase has come so cheaply that the hammer price is a bargain.

But he is dismayed when the bottle that holds the ghost of the young girl stirs the room, the price rising in ten-per-cent-increments that quickly leap into the thousands. Determined to complete a set, he outbids everyone, claiming, at last, the young girl's spirit, regretting nothing about the enormous cost.

At first, he displays the bottles on a living-room shelf like trophies. A few visitors laugh, and he smiles patiently. When, inevitably, someone asks, "How do you know which is which?" he says, "By looking closely." When everyone, before they leave, asks what he's paid, he answers, "I never discuss business." One night, a woman touches the young girl's bottle, beginning to lift it, and he tells her to put it down in a tone that makes her husband say, "Wow. Just wow."

The next day, he moves the bottles to his bedroom, replacing the originals with facsimiles. After he tells a friend that the ghosts are happier now that they feel safe, the news of the fake bottles spreads until he has the house to himself.

He coddles them, trying to coax them visible, setting the bottles where the morning light will strike them as early as possible. He is patient, giving them time to recognize he is no longer selfish, that he understands their privacy is important. Someone, he believes, must have threatened to shatter those bottles, furious because the ghosts refused to reveal themselves. When their miracles were put up for auction, they must have arrived like the adopted from a foreign orphanage where fear was as persistent as an arctic winter.

He listens for voices. He watches for the light within to change. He encourages the faint fog of breath by lowering the temperature of his bedroom, squinting for the possibility of the tiniest of etchings that will transcribe the unspoken desires of the dead, the differences age and gender make in their afterlives.

Months pass. Then years. At last, he carries those prizes to bed each night and lies awake in the dark, pressing the glass to his chest, devoted now to dreaming of uncapping those bottles, the girl's first, joyous, the incredible brief breath of escape brushing across his face. Then the old man's, how his flurry will teach him the importance of what he once purchased--observing the future, tracking the invisible to discern just where the dead disappear to when they are freed.

Prom Weekend

After she hung up her new prom dress, her father wanted to know who was taking her. "Dennis," she said.

"Does Dennis have a last name?" he said.

"Sirikawa."

"A Japanese boy? Absolutely not."

Her father had been in the war, but he'd fought in Europe, not the Pacific. She'd gone out with a boy with a German name. He lived three blocks away, not far from where Dennis lived. "You will not leave this house. I'll make sure of that. He can knock on the door all night."

"His parents are Japanese. He's American."

"That's what he thinks."

He made her call. He stood beside her like a home invader, telling her to talk normal and make it short. "No crying on the phone," he said. "Promise me. Just a simple 'Sorry, I can't.'"

There was one phone in the house. In the kitchen. Plugged into the wall. He stood by the sink while she kept her promise. After she hung up, he said, "Another boy asked you. Your mother bragged about it. You know how she talks. When she said one was Japanese, it sounded like she thought you'd caught some kind of special fish. Call the other one. You want to wear that dress, right? That dress is pretty, right?"

Yes, she thought it was. A white, flower-print, sleeveless top sewn into a long pink skirt. She'd put off telling the other boy "no," saying she might not be allowed to go, that her father didn't like the idea of her going into the city at night, being driven there by a boy he didn't know, all of which was true. She'd promised to call because she was embarrassed to say it to his face.

She'd wished he hadn't asked her. Now she wished she was somebody who didn't call him and say "yes" and listen to his joy for a minute while her father smoked and watched television in the living room. Her mother said, "Maybe Dennis will think you picked Michael just because."

"Maybe he'll think it's because we celebrate V-J Day every year," she said.

"Don't be so sarcastic," her mother said, but the girl was already crying because she knew that it was true.

Michael's first and last name combination was so common, there were three others in the high school. One was even in the senior class, their brand-new 1966 yearbook photos side by side with middle initials included to tell them apart. Her date came first because his initial was A. Both of their haircuts were the same as the one Dennis had in his photo two pages later.

Her father made sure to find work to do in the front yard until Michael with the American name walked to the door with a corsage in one hand. She told her mother, "Just one picture" and kept her hands to her sides the way she did when she was posed beside cousins at Thanksgiving.

She danced with Michael six times, never two songs in a row. During the third song, "Yesterday," she began to hate him when he tugged her close. Dennis wasn't there.

She let him kiss her goodnight. When she pulled away, pointing to the porch light, he smiled as if she were making a promise for the future in code.

Her saying "Yes" had included a post-prom trip to an amusement park the following morning. A Sunday, but her father excused her from church "just this one time." She locked the front door and went upstairs to her room to finish dressing. For fifteen minutes, she watched from her window until his car pulled into the driveway.

She stepped back from the window, nearly to the closet where the prom dress she loved hung in the center. She listened until Michael with the initial A knocked on her door. She could not see him from where she stood, but she held her breath and waited until he knocked again, louder this time.

She'd kept her promise to be ready at 11:15 a.m. He had been right on time. And now he knocked longer than she imagined any boy ever would for her. At last, she sat on her bed and waited, eyes closed, for him to hate her, too.

After January's Active Shooter Drill

. . . the substitute teacher said, It's time for science now. The weather unit. Don't grumble, children. Listen closely. Winter is like a great-grandmother who will visit infrequently at first, then not at all.

Don't cry. Be happy to wear your clumsy boots and mittens while she is still with you. Your snowmen, though, are crawling north like bark beetles, those refugees who will slaughter your forests like a swarm of saws.

Don't look at the clock. Thousands of miles from here, the ice is thinning. Even at the North Pole, a meltwater lake has formed. In Greenland, in just one day, twelve billion tons of ice has melted.

Now, shut your eyes. Good. I'll bet you thought the weather unit would be boring, right? Especially, last year, when the worst was twelve above zero and the tornadoes were just news from Mississippi and Alabama, 700 miles away. And this year, you've had school every day, not one delay, nothing close to a snow day. But don't you be fooled. The weather has weapons.

No peeking. Sit up and listen. In less than a day, sixty-eight inches of rain has fallen, and the fastest foot of rain, forty-two minutes, was in Missouri, not far. Stop fidgeting. In July, a blizzard has swept the Great Plains, only a bit farther; for Christmas Eve, in Montana, a drop of eighty-four degrees. Scary, right? School shooter stuff. All those Montana kiddies in flimsy jackets, thinking winter was on holiday.

Stop waving your hands. I know those are the things that happen less often than a gun coming to school. Your weather forecast, though, is for clouds. Don't interrupt. There's no telling what might be coming. Be prepared. You Boy Scouts don't know the half of it. Girls, too—wipe those smiles off your faces. While you work on your merit badges, the night will stay noon-hot. Your fathers and mothers will hide what they're afraid of like men who dress in masks and camouflage.

In the worst weather, you're on your own. Don't look at me like that. Once upon a time, the year all of you started school, a wildfire leveled a town called Paradise to a stencil for hell. Don't oooh and aaah like that, you know that's true. And this year, fires are ravaging the Arctic. The wind, children, loves embers so much it sometimes carries them safely for miles. Always check to see what's tumbling and floating with the seeds and spores you'll learn about in another unit. Those pretty things will descend by chance to where destruction can root and prosper.

Every last one of you know what I'm talking about, don't you? The drill you need for active-weather needs to be held as often as brushing your teeth. Tomorrow, we'll have a full hour. Tomorrow, be absolutely still, children. Tomorrow, hold your breath and keep your eyes shut until I say *open*.

THE GUEST-CLOSET BALL

After his wife dies, he discovers her bowling ball. Why, he wonders, had she owned a ball when she never, not once, had bowled? How long had she owned it? Not once had she mentioned bowling, and yet the ball, he is certain, had been drilled especially for her grip. His fingers barely squeeze in, his thumb is impossible to fit.

And such an expensive-looking bag to carry it in. The ball, pale blue and sparkling with metallic-white threads, is sealed in a shell-like protective case. Among the thirty other pairs arranged in the closet, he discovers a pair of shoes like the ones he remembers from bowling twice as a boy. They are almost like slippers, the soles designed to promote sliding. Unlike the bag and ball, they show signs of wear.

They had been married for twenty-five years, childless at their silver anniversary, but no sign that they wouldn't make it to the golden one until she collapsed two months later, an aneurysm in her brain. The case was under her summer clothes in the spare closet she used to store them, exchanging her outfits according to season. Was it hidden or forgotten? The question follows him for days. He asks her friends. He questions her brother. Everyone claims they had never seen her bowl, never heard her talk about bowling.

Maybe she just enjoyed it like a brief vacation. Like going to the movies alone, what he's done for decades. Or she had given it up when they were married, something she could live without. Though he wonders why anyone who'd invested in bowling, buying the shoes that could be rented, the ball that the alleys supplied for free. They seem as essential as a pair of boots for winter, a pair for jogging, a pair for mornings in the nearby fitness room.

He drives to the nearest bowling alley, less than two miles and yet he doesn't even remember the name until he pulls into the lot. Best Bowl, the sign brags, excusing him.

He shows her photo to the middle-aged attendant, who studies the picture then shakes his head. "I'd remember that pretty face," he finally says. As if he's searching for a missing person, he shows the photo to the bowlers who are using only six of the thirty-two lanes.

Maybe, he thinks, she traveled to a place farther away, keeping her bowling a secret by being a stranger. He drives to another in the next town. Classic Lanes, the sign says, as if promising nostalgia. When no one recognizes her from the photo, he watches two men bowl an entire game and checks the time. As they begin another, he wonders how his wife could have found so many secret minutes. A sign advertises all-night bowling—midnight to 6 a.m.—something, done alone, that sounds impossible. Fifty games. Maybe sixty or, unimaginably, more.

Closure, he thinks, is a tenuous thing, but he drives to a third, the last of the lanes within thirty miles. Sunset Bowl. "Maybe," the woman at the desk says. He studies her until she says, "I can't say for sure, so probably no," but he feels certain.

He pays for a pair of red-and-green shoes and finds a ball that accepts his fingers and thumb. It's not hard to keep the ball on the narrow lane, six or more pins falling every time he throws a first ball. What's hard is scattering all ten or knocking over the few that remain with the second shot.

The score is kept automatically for everyone to see. After ten frames, he has two x's and three slashes and 138. Two lanes away, a woman is bowling with a man who is as quiet as a long-time husband. From where he sits, he sees her score is 142, but she has two more frames yet to fill. He watches her release her orange ball, the way her breasts lift as she extends her arm, how her skirt rides up her thighs. A woman bowling is a beautiful thing, he thinks, unlacing his clown-colored, rented shoes.

WHILE HE STILL DRIVES HIS FATHER'S CAR

The boy remembers that a few miles from where he is speeding, at Keller's Auto Body, his town's latest death car sits twisted and torn, dumped, for now, where traffic can creep past with exclamations and cameras. He has read the reports, how some half-drunk, careless driver his age was the one who escaped from that totaled car with non-life-threatening injuries.

The boy wonders if every town, even one as small as his, needs such a homemade Fatal Accident Museum. For a moment, he slows, imagining that accidents are forming all along the back road and there is no way to warn the oncoming drivers his age who are sober yet changing a station or texting or resting one hand on the thigh of a girl who, like he is, unbuckled, nothing, despite air bags, to keep either of them from being thrown from a tumbling car.

The boy knows the girl who died. Beginning a month ago, for three weekends, she was willing to ride, sometimes unbuckled, while he raced on this highway. Six nights, altogether, she walked safely into her parents' house without an accident arriving, his speed and carelessness and a curve not forcing her scream into his ear.

Now, approaching the crash site, he imagines being someone who drives here to retrace this stretch of highway with his needle set exactly at the estimated speed that's been published. At once, he hates that person enough to turn off the radio and do nothing but obey the speed limit as he drives that road up and back, then up and back again without that girl who was his passenger when he was speeding, not sober, yet safe.

The boy's passenger is the terror that swells as he passes her driveway four times like a late-adolescent honor guard. It moves closer as he slows below the posted limit to examine that house he approached but never entered. It presses against him as he remembers leaving her, the last time, at the door like an estranged, embarrassed brother, her next-weekend accident looming "just around the bend and over the next hill" like a war zone occupied by the young and conscripted.

HAPPY ENDINGS

This much was certain—because of the mess it left, the bear had been eating from a dumpster behind the Rib House just before it was electrocuted. The bus boys claimed it climbed the power pole because it was frightened by a dog. "The dog was still hanging around," they told me. "That black lab. What else could scare a bear up a pole like that and then not be run off by it tumbling down all scorched to hell and back."

I wrote whatever they babbled down. I was there for rock radio WOOM, not the newspaper or the police, so I let them elaborate and embellish any way they wanted. A bystander who said he was hunter guessed the bear weighed one hundred and fifty pounds. The dog I saw looked to be about seventy-five, so it seemed to me the bear lacked spirit. And now it lacked everything, smoked the way it was from crawling onto the cross bar and taking however many volts run through those lines.

It was a better story to cover than most in Moorefield, but I admit a good reporter would fact check something like that, put the number of volts in his story, but WOOM's listeners didn't care. They wanted to hear the voices of people they might recognize and details about the burned body of the bear during the three minutes of stories we snuck in before the hour, running it up to when every other station broke for news, their listeners maybe switching to where they knew music was playing instead of voices.

Those bus boys had a peach of a story to tell, and I had them on tape. "First the lights flickered," one said. "Something you can't have in a restaurant. And second, we were going out back to smoke no matter if it was World War III starting up because we got our break right then. And there's no missing any kind of bear, don't need to be no grizzly, when it's laying at the bottom of the electric pole at the edge of your parking lot and all crisped like he'd walked slowly through fire."

"One more mess we weren't getting stuck with at least," said the other guy, older than forty by the look of him, a bad age to be a bus boy. "We just walked up to that bear like men who believed dead was dead and there wasn't anything like resurrection or second chances in this world."

WOOM kept that story going. It was better than a hundred-dollar jackpot phone-in promo to spruce up the ratings, and I did my part by talking that bear up as long as I could. Our listeners knew the dee-jays would get that bear into their patter between rock blocks, laughing about how Rib House patrons might think twice about parking behind the restaurant without checking over their heads.

The newspaper version, it turned out, got picked up by the wire service and started appearing in city papers, and then, a week later, Saturday Night Live's *Weekend Update* milked some laughs from it. A long time to stay in any kind of news as entertainment cycle, but that wasn't the end of it until my mother called her two cents in over the phone so long after the event that I thought she read about it in a monthly magazine.

"That bear's story is a tearjerker, for sure. People love a good cry. After a while, people get tired always hearing about how Jesus rose from the dead. That one about John the Baptist is a better story. Like all the rest of us, he doesn't get a second chance. I never understood why he doesn't get more publicity."

"People want happy endings, Mom. I think you're wrong."

"Angels? Rescue? That's so boring. If that bear falls off the pole and is still alive and nursed back to health, it's nothing more than gossip. And afraid of a dog, they say? That big thing afraid of something half his size? I knew somebody just like that, and you would have known him, too, if he hadn't run off with his imaginary angel, a story so old that nobody would ever report it. But that bear frying like a serial killer on the hot seat is news and then some, a tale to tell everybody you know."

Hansel

Drainage pipes had been set in place to accommodate the demands of sixty new families in the housing plan being built behind Terry's street. Hardly any houses were finished, and none of them were occupied, so those huge pipes, not yet in use, looked to him like adventure.

The model home that had been built before any of the lots were sold was unlocked from nine to five. "That's for the wives of men who wear suits to work," his father said. "In a few years, those women will want a bigger house, and then they'll be gone and people like us will live in what they leave behind." When Terry said nothing, his father added, "You'll stay out of those pipes if you know what's good for you."

What Terry did, at first, was crawl only until one pipe connected to another larger one. He knew that the pipes would intersect and grow wider until there were only the two he could see from the narrow back road his father used as a short cut home. They gaped high up on the hillside above the Flats, where houses were neither new nor nice. "Those folks in the Flats, they'll barely notice. That creek down there floods every house come March. Some unlucky day, a few will get swept away."

Soon, Terry crabwalked through the larger storm drains, pretending to be following a tunnel to where treasure had been hidden centuries ago. "One of those old mine shafts down there by the Flats is going to swallow a boy someday," his father said the next time they took the short cut. As if he was Hansel's smarter cousin, Terry started to drop small stones while he crawled. Now he would never get lost.

One afternoon, as if his mother was taking a tour, Terry sat on the black-and-white zigzag-patterned couch inside the model home. He watched two women brush their finger-tips over the slick Braille of appliances before they parted the gold and green patterned drapes as if they loved the view of construction and rain. When the house, at last, stood empty, he opened the refrigerator, but all the packages and boxes inside were empty.

Afterward, he crab-walked far enough to nearly stand. There was light ahead, hazy with heavy rain lit up repeatedly by lightning. He felt water swirling past and over his shoes and made sure to stop a few feet before the pipe ended. He wanted to sit, but the water ran ankle high now. For what seemed like a long time, he kept his arms spread, each hand pressing against a rounded wall.

When, at last, the rain stopped, Terry took two small steps, just far enough to see the Flats below him, a few back yards full of old tires, abandoned cars, and a scattering of swing sets and slides. He wasn't close enough to the pipe's end to see the hill drop so steeply beneath him he thought he would fall almost to the Flats, landing on the narrow road unless the undergrowth of scrubby trees and bushes caught him, all that thorny, jagged crap that he couldn't name, stuff that seemed like it would never grow high enough to block the mouth of the pipe.

Terry turned, ready to retrace his path, and there was enough light for him to notice how a patch of small stones had collected where he'd been standing, enough that he knew the geography of the buried pipes must have been scrubbed by the rushing water. He remembered that the last turn had been an angled left. The next Y might have split in either direction.

He began to sweat and swear his mild, fourth-grade oaths like "damn" and "hell" and "shit" until he could hear his father saying, "Shut up and think for a minute," and he did, listening as if the world in the dark ahead of him was a house larger than any he'd ever been inside. "This way," he said to himself when he came to each choice. All he had to do was make sure the pipes grew smaller until he needed to crawl.

II

Two Short Stories in Flash

Boxing the Future

Peace

All of the fathers but the boy's have souvenirs from the war--helmets, guns, a bayonet etched, sometimes, in German, Italian, or the strange, unknowable Japanese. One father has shrapnel in his back. One flings an open hand for failures. One keeps bottles in his garage and car. All of them carry cigarettes and depend upon blasphemy for speech. The boy's apartment has none of those things. Not whiskey. not even the cigarettes and curses. Year by year, his father stays silent, vanished beneath a distant, sealed door. The boys who live nearby point those foreign guns at each other. Because whoever had fired them is dead, they tumble, quiver, and lie still. Because the boy has no weapon except stealth, he becomes a traitor they execute.

Summoned

One afternoon, the boy is lost in the public pool locker room, old enough to know his mother is not searching by methodically counting down the lockers, eliminating one row after another to find him. He is embarrassed, not terrified, not yet, except of admitting helplessness to half-dressed or naked men, their bodies so impossibly hairy or fat that the boy, smooth and skinny, could never belong to them.

The boy's wet suit clings clammy as fever flesh. His mother, who loves to swim, had changed elsewhere. She had talked his face into the water, lifting his legs into the miracle of floating. When she let go, he had panicked into splash and flounder. Now, by loudspeaker, the boy hears himself summoned, his name and age repeated just before a voice says, "Your mother is waiting for you outside the door through the blue and yellow wall."

The nearest naked man says, "That you, son?" but the boy shakes his head as if he can't be lost. As if there are other boys alone among the rows of lockers who need to find their way by colors.

Head down, the boy studies the floor as he walks away from where his mother waits. He turns into a vacant row of lockers and begins to count. Before long, he is somewhere else, someone not almost seven and helpless while strangers examine him, amused by the happy end of a mother's terror. When he reaches sixty, the boy walks toward the door along the puddled corridor near the open showers where men are busy with their bodies, the rush of spray smothering their hearing as he passes by like a boy who, unashamed, is about to peel off his suit and stand naked among them.

Maze

The boy's school is noise and nuns, as simple as a sidewalk broken by numbered streets, but Mass is an unsolvable labyrinth of soloed Latin. Every day, after school, he creates a maze, each, he tells his mother, a new version of purgatory. When he completes it, he asks her to escape without lifting her pencil.

They live alone, the studio apartment small enough to

memorize, the corridors on each floor straight and right-angled, a toddler's puzzle. When his mother struggles, retracing, he imagines her prayer. When she exits, he believes she has managed penance. Always, he times her.

One evening, his mother, the pencil still pressed to the paper, declares there is no solution. Mute, he taps his watch. The apartment is cluttered with hesitation and sighs. When she retraces again, the line thickens until it fills each alley, until it's hell.

Overnight

"You've been here before," the boy's grandmother says, "when your Momma was carrying you." When he asks where his mother has gone, leaving him behind for his first overnight, his grandmother says, "To the land of privacy."

"There's no such place," the boy says, but his grandmother presses a finger to his lips, nudging him through a bedroom door with her other hand.

"Your Daddy took a nap here right before he left for the war," she says. "Your Momma woke him when the time came, and then he was gone."

Just like that, the boy thinks, but his grandmother doesn't stop. "I've kept it just the same as your Momma made it back up that early morning. Never washed a thing, the same sheets and pillowcase waiting for him." She takes a breath and pats his head. "Now," she says. "You."

The boy locks the door. He sleeps on the floor. In the morning, before it is fully light, he wakes and unlocks the door to leave for the bathroom down the hall. When he returns, his grandmother is in the bedroom. She says, "My, first thing, without asking, you made the bed as perfect as she did that day. Your Momma has taught you well."

When his mother returns, she hugs his grandmother and hurries him to the car. After she asks how the night went, he tells her he was afraid. "That's natural," she says. "It's something new, and now you'll be fine."

"I locked the door," he says, and his mother smiles.

"Privacy already?" she says. "You're too smart for your age, but I'll tell Grandma about that and next time you won't have to."

"I slept on the floor."

He feels the car speed up as if they have to hurry. A green sign says that within the next six miles there are exits to three towns, two with long names he doesn't know how to pronounce. "What did Grandma say to you?" his mother says.

"This is your Daddy's bed."

"You already knew that."

The boy rubs his thumbs against his fingers. "She said it's never been touched."

"Since then?"

He turns his thumbs so the nails are scratching him. "These are his sheets," the boy says. "This is his pillowcase."

"She said 'is'?"

"Yes," he says. He wants to ask which exit will take them to the land of privacy. He presses as hard as he can, but he can't make himself bleed.

During the Epidemic

The boy brings a dime every Friday to slide into a slot inside a card featuring a smiling girl on crutches. He loves seeing his card fill up. When there are ten dimes, he starts again on a card with a crippled boy. Sister Rose, his third-grade teacher, keeps everyone's cards inside her desk. "You wash your hands, all of you," she says, after the class slots their dimes. "There's no telling who handled those coins. How filthy he was and what you could catch."

Every day, just after lunch, Sister Rose inspects their desks. They need to be clean. No crumbs inside or out, spotless before they have public health, which is, Sister Rose says, a lifesaving class. The contagious, she explains, leave filth that hides on buses and streetcars and seats at the movies. You'll never know who's been there and given you the itch and fester. The contagious never cover their mouths when they sneeze. They wipe their noses on their sleeves where crusts collect like scabs that bleed. They borrow combs and touch fountains with their mouths."

When the boy raises his hand and asks a question, she talks as if he's told her time is up. "You won't know who they are until they carry that filth to you like flies. Look around. You'll see what I mean. Eyes open, class. Keep yourselves clean. Filth is a welcome mat for polio."

When June is close, she says, "Polio doesn't go away like chicken pox or the measles. You wear braces and use crutches like poor Richard Hartman, who's missed so much school he'll fall a year behind." As always, when everybody looks at Richard Hartman's empty desk, the boy touches his desktop as if filth has returned while he listened.

"Look at this photograph," Sister Rose says on the last day of school, walking up and down the aisles so everyone can see. "Those children are stuck forever in iron lungs. Those children will never do anything but lie inside them so they can breathe." She pauses by Richard Hartman's empty desk and says, "One last time, remember to keep clean."

All summer, the boy washes his hands before lunch and dinner. He cleans his crumbs off the table before his mother sees them. He floats inside an inner tube in the county park lake, careful not to drift where the water would be over his head. Jerry Mushik, who sat beside him all year, splashes and swallows the water as if the contagious never peed there. He says Sister Rose isn't their teacher anymore, but she'll have Richard Hartman again next year and have to shut up about polio every day he isn't absent.

In September, Richard Hartman, wearing leg braces and using crutches, is still with the boy's class. Miss Gardiner, who is younger than his mother, never checks their desks after lunch, but she has new March of Dimes cards for each of them, even Richard Hartman. "The dimes aren't going to help that boy," his mother says. "It's too late for that."

Jerry Mushik laughs when the boy washes his hands after he inserts his first dime. Mushik puts his on his tongue and closes his mouth. "Fuck polio," he whispers. For the next three weeks, Mushik licks his dime. In October, in the cloak room before school, Mushik forces two third-grade boys to lick their dimes, and neither of them get sick.

Boxing

The boy's mother notices that a heavy bag has been hung from a basement beam. "Someone I know would want you to do this," she says, after she buys the boy boxing gloves and has him watch the Friday night fights with her on their tiny television. "See?" she says, but when he touches that bag with the gloves, he inhales as if sinking in sand. "On your toes," his mother says. "The future is furious, a full-time thug. It wants more than you have, so you must learn to juke and shuffle."

When he hesitates, his mother talks like she's broadcasting. "Jab," she says. "Discover weakness. Uppercut, body blows, the hook from your left instead of the right you too much rely on. With or without brains, tomorrow is a brute."

Nothing is more serious than the speed bag she hangs in their studio. "Again," she says. "Now." His shoes skid where his father's absence lies slick and oily on the floor. In every corner are the things unused for years—vow and promise, faith and joy—each tangled among his father's pre-war clothes. Fear loiters near the locked door, its glowing cigarette a clock. She tells him to breathe as he shadow-boxes. "Listen," she says, "that voice you will hear is the undefeated singing."

Rehearsals

Early in the first summer of the Salk vaccine, the boy lives with his aunt in New Jersey for a week. It will be summer camp, but free and without the strangers, his mother explains, pointing out the nearby forest and lake, pressing him toward a cousin his age who loves chess. He squeals and laughs when he tells the boy to tip his king after every game. When they walk in the forest, they follow a path. Whether they enter the woods or not, his aunt, each night, examines them for ticks. After his cousin tells his mother the boy left the path and found an abandoned cabin, they never walk there again. For the week, they share not one embedded tick.

Though neither of them can swim, they go to the lake daily. The water turns their bodies brown. "Like rust," his aunt says. "It washes off." Both of them keep their heads above water. Their lips sealed.

On the last late afternoon, firemen arrive at the lake. With a bullhorn and uniforms, they order everyone out of the water. His aunt says, "They're going to drag the lake," and he watches two of them sling and lower a grappling hook while a man who looks older than his grandfather nudges the boat into tight loops with his oars. A monthly exercise, only practice, his aunt says, but even with the sun still shining, he and his cousin shiver, dry inside their towels, but a chill clinging to their groins. At last, the firemen bring up a body, its arms and legs limp, lake water pouring, then dripping as they reach to embrace it, securing the dead to applause from the shore.

What ends that week is a bus ride from New Jersey to Pittsburgh, his aunt placing him in the front window seat, closing her goodbye with "Stay put and be quiet." A sailor, moments later, settles next to him with a quintet of comic books, all of them featuring miracles and war. The boy wishes he could tell him the story about floating above the make-believe dead. One by one, as he finishes them, the sailor hands those battles for countries and planets to the boy. Someone dies violently in every story. When the boy finishes each story, he pages backward to examine the bodies.

At Howard Johnson's, near Harrisburg, the sailor buys the boy potato chips and a Mound's Bar, escorts him to the men's room where nothing happens, that episode so ordinary, the boy doesn't mention it in Pittsburgh where his mother says how proud she is, how he looks bigger after a week away, healthier, too. They wait for his suitcase to be extracted from beneath the bus. He opens it to prove he's lost nothing she has trusted him with.

"I have a surprise," his mother says. When she parks in front of a row house double, she says, "One side is ours. All your things are already inside." She guides him through five open doors until she nods at the one that is closed. Inside is a bed and a chest of drawers that fill half the space. "You need your own room," she says, but he shakes his head and backs away. "What?" she says. "All of our furniture is used."

"It's Dad's," the boy says, and there is nothing she can say that convinces him it is not, that she would never do that to him. What she does is drive him fifty miles to see that the bed is still exactly where his father left it, his grandmother saying, "Yes. Yes, it is," like a defendant before his mother drives him back to the bed that is his own.

Tomorrow is his next shot in the Salk sequence, sixteen days until his birthday. Double digits, his mother says, as if it is a difficult milestone, something achieved, with practice, like a column of report card As, something like surviving serious wounds.

Them! . . . and . . . Tarantula!

"Remember this!" his mother says. Across from the Home

stead Theater, the sidewalk swarms with strikers buzzing *hell* and *damn* while she buys their way inside where huge ants, within minutes, are screaming at flame throwers, working their claws as they burn. "The End" signals they have entered an hour late, but in minutes, a huge spider stalks the screaming until it, too, is fire-bombed, this time from a jet.

The previews promise two comedies, double westerns, paired romances. When the ants return, his mother mutters, "We know what happens to Them," and tugs the boy to the door beside the screen. Over his head, a woman ten times his size stands hypnotized by a set of enormous eyes. His mother, when he turns, is waving from the lobby.

Outside, at twilight, the strike-closed mill has turned as radioactive as a test-site emptied by the bomb. Lifting their signs, the men spread into traffic. "Them!" his mother says, as if steelworkers were giants, as if an army would soon destroy them all.

The Nuclear Age

On television, the Head Groundsman at Stonehenge trims the lawn with a push mower like the men in the row houses use on their patches of grass. He rolls up the sleeves of his white Oxford, a shirt like the one the boy wears only on Sundays, freshly washed, starched and ironed. His mother says the Groundsman is making the grass perfect for the tourists who will arrive for solstice.

A month ago, a man who lived across the street had died. Yesterday, the boy's mother had shown him the push mower in the dead man's garage and told him to mow what was becoming a tiny meadow of dandelion, thistle, goldenrod, and milkweed. She had reminded him to store it exactly where he'd found it in the dead man's garage. "Sweep up after yourself," she said. "Make it look like it hasn't been used."

At Stonehenge, the Head Groundsman says he loves his ancient church. He trims the base of the miraculous construction, meticulous in each shadow. When the crowds arrive, nothing will be out of place. By now, the boy believes the Bible is only a book of stories. Church is a chore he does poorly. Everything will outlive me is what he never says to the priest.

The next Sunday evening, the boy reads about the villages abandoned in the Soviet Union, the ones whose names have been erased from maps. He knows the villagers are dead or dying in places as mysterious as radiation or ancient relics. By now, the tourists have finished listening for ghosts, leaving behind a clean, well-tended cathedral.

Smart-Alecks

Sister Miriam's desk is in the back of the room so she can keep an eye out. In her black dress, she walks an aisle from back to front, then loops around the row of desks by the blackboard and comes down another aisle. "A good shaking is what some of you need," she says as she walks. She means all of the fifth-grade boys. She uses the shoulder grab and the arm squeeze, the wrist tug and the hand clenched on the backs of their necks. She never touches a girl.

Outside, during recess, the boy laughs when Ronnie Tomlin says they should shake the shit out of each other. One boy grabs another and shakes while the girls stare. The boy twists the chains on one of the six playground swings and lifts his feet, spinning like crazy. When a girl says she wants to try, he twists the chains for her and she squeals as she spins.

The next morning, Sister Miriam shows the class pictures of the asylum seats a doctor once built to shake some sense into lunatics. Not so long ago, she says, those chairs hung from hospital ceilings. They shook out the madness. They spun for hours to lessen the blood to the brain.

At recess, an hour later, the boy and five others sit on the swings, twisting their steel chains around and around and tight until somebody shoves, and they scream and spin and thrash like crazy. "Smart-alecks," Sister Miriam says, when they come back to class. "Know-it-alls," standing so close the boy can feel her breath on the back of his head when she shakes him while he sits in his hard-backed seat screwed into the floor. "Do you feel good sense getting into that crazy brains of yours?" she says, but the boy, facing forward, nods because sometimes he thinks he's crazy.

That night, the boy's mother says Angie Bechtold's mother is on the news. "Ruby Bechtold was a funny one," his mother says. "She had her own ways of doing things."

Angie Bechtold is absent in the morning. The class listen while Sister Miriam tells them to be considerate when Angie returns. Mary Russo raises her hand and asks, "What's *considerate* mean?"

"That's when you act extra nice to somebody because a person she loves has died."

The day Angie returns to school Ronnie Tomlin spins on the swings but doesn't yell anything. Everyone waits for a turn to spin, even Angie. They are all considerate, everybody quiet while they spin and spin.

Buddy System

Twelve years old, beside someone named Len he barely knows, the boy drowns himself in the church camp lake, both of them watching each other for panic or surrender while they stand where their heads nearly crown the surface. No one notices them resurface, but Len is the first to grasp the dock and pull himself up, holding on while the boy counts to eleven before he surfaces.

Neither of them can swim. Carefully, hand over hand along the dock's slippery railroad ties, they had crept to where a white 6 is painted on the highest tie. A flurry of boys who swim had ignored them while they held hands and let go, sinking until they had stood one step from safety.

Now, neither looks at the other as they work back to the white 4 where an orange-beaded rope stretches to the opposite dock. The lake follows them, shy and silent, to their cabin where it puddles outside, waiting to trail them to dinner, lapping at their feet while they swallow meatloaf and baked beans, drink the sweet, metallic orangeade.

Later, outdoors for a sermon surrounded by evening hymns, the lake ripples between them while they lip-sync. When its waves dampen their shoes, they inch closer together, their knees touching. The boys on either side of them sing each verse of every hymn in a falsetto near helium-squeak that sounds trapped as a damaged soul.

After lights-out, the lake deepens by their beds. In the

dark, it soaks their sheets with stories that begins, "Underwater, the seconds stretch into a scream." Its spray shimmers where thin moonlight seeps through a small, sealed window, its voice now hoarse, then going so thick the words reach them like tongues seeking their bodies to be sure they are not alone.

Two days later, when his mother drives him home, she asks whether he has finally learned to swim, and the boy says, "Yes."

The Scientific Method

In July, its leash twisted by an hour of pacing, a neighbor's beagle leaps off his half of the porch and hangs itself. In August, a sixth-grade classmate, swimming alone, slips under the murky surface of a strip mine pool. In September, the boy is starting junior high in a public school, everybody in his home room a stranger.

Before long, Sputnik says he might soon be a Communist. Before long, the Asian Flu half-empties his classes. By November, the Soviets are listening to Laika, their space dog, until she smothers into silence, circling the earth until she plummets into re-entry's furnace.

That week, the boy crawls into his mother's closet and sits among dresses stacked for charity. With the thinnest negligee, he seals the space where light creeps in and waits for what the air will teach him. For an orbit's ninety minutes, he rides weightless in that capsule.

When he re-opens the door and stands, he sees the speed bag is lying behind a blanket on the closet shelf, but he does not touch it. Downstairs, his mother is still ironing. The radio plays Johnny Mathis followed by Frank Sinatra, both melodies so familiar the boy mouths the words as he descends to earth.

In early December, Chuck Kress, who lives in the double next door, pledges to count only to ninety before he opens the door to the freezer left behind in a nearby empty house. As soon as the boy shuts himself inside, back curled and knees puled tight in a space more suitable for a dog, he starts his own count, concentrating on that metronome for breath.

His heart thrums in his ears, graphing itself against darkness like the strikes of an EKG. He presses one hand between his legs, holding fear, refusing to touch anything but himself while he calculates the mathematics of air. He has reached one hundred and twenty-two when the face of Chuck Kress explains who he has become.

When the boy says he'd counted way past ninety, Chuck Kress says he counted like a launch commander, a man with the job of watching a clock, no longer considering the astronaut who, after all, was only a passenger. The boy slides the shelves back into place as if they are the covers over unmarked wells, ending the experimental age, which he knows wasn't science at all, just the anecdotal evidence of fantasy's tiny risk and the chatter of his senses.

The Day of the Triffids

The boy turns thirteen, summer stuffed with science fiction movies and books, the unpaved road below the house split along the shoulder, guardrails slumping level with the gravel. Nearby, a dump deepens with tires and trash, appliances, mattresses. Beyond it, the state game land is a place, when entered, to gather fear like berries. When leaves smother the sky, he is underwater; when branches snap, the played-out mines are graves, his mother's "Never alone in there" insistent as a fire alarm.

In July, he is in love with the Triffids, the alien trees that advance like guerillas after the world goes blind from watching a meteor shower. The forest becomes malignant. The Triffids flourish in the Earth's soil and have an appetite for all those sightless humans. He has watched it twice.

The paths he follows in the game lands are half-eaten by locust and sumac. Just outside of their boundaries, mine entrances are labeled like poisons; a thin canal carries runoff to dunes of silt.

On screen, the Triffids are so easily killed by salt water, they might have arrived from West Oz. The world is saved. Every tree in the woods is rooted or dead. But when August begins, the boy reads the novel, where nothing in the final scenes ends those aliens, even on the last page.

One late afternoon, among a thick stand of pine trees, the boy finds a striped shirt and black socks soaked and faintly rotten as if they have wintered there. The shirt hangs so small in his hands, that whoever had worn it begins to scream. The boy listens hard for heavy steps. He checks the trees for movement.

Although nothing happens except fantasy following him home, he picks up a heavy branch and carries it toward the road, clutching it like bravery. In his room, the novel still lying beside his bed, the boy closes his eyes and sits in his wooden chair that strangers have cut and shaped and fitted into something so common that one would always surround him. He keeps his eyes pressed tightly shut until he cries.

Good Things

*R*aunchy is a word the boy doesn't recognize, but he is in love with how loud his neighbor Chuck Kress turns up that song on the radio in his spotless used car. Especially the saxophone, what the boy dreams of playing.

Chuck Kress is sixteen and taking him for a spin, two miles up and two miles back on the familiar road that runs so straight and flat, Chuck can reach 100 on the speedometer. "Buried," Chuck says, laughing, though they are down to sixty, their street a quarter mile away, when a car backs across both lanes from a roadside garage. Chuck brakes hard, the Chevy four-wheel-drifting toward a row of junipers that fill the passenger-side window as the boy grips the door handle and braces, the world turning dark green just before it brightens, Chuck's car spinning and stopping so close to the one straddling the road that the boy can see the shape of that stranger's inaudible scream.

Neither of them make a sound during those moments of lost control. *Raunchy* fades into a deejay's voice, but they still do not speak while the other driver straightens and drives away. Chuck, when he talks as he turns into their street, says, "Good thing I knew what to do." The boy says nothing because he has no idea what Chuck has done to save them. To himself, he says, *Good thing I didn't open the door.*

Chuck's dog, chained outside, barks as the boy gets out of

the car. "You won't forget this one," Chuck says. "Not ever." The boy doesn't even nod. "Say 'thank you' the next time you see me," Chuck calls after him. The boy's mother is at work. He creeps to his room and huddles on his bed.

Long after the boy lies down, Chuck's miserable dog keeps up with its yammering. The boy's quiet hysteria gradually fades. Remembering his hand about to yank the door handle, he thinks, *Good thing I hadn't had an extra second to act. Good thing I didn't have time enough to do what was worst. Good thing that lesson was a private one. Good thing I hadn't spouted that wrong answer out loud.* He makes a vow of a future filled with caution, something that sounds, at once, like it has been copied from the answers someone else is writing for an exam he is not prepared for. Like he has been caught cheating, and the teacher is furious.

THE TIMES

Home

After the locks are changed, after he stops cursing and pounding on both doors, he hurls his key against the kitchen window while McCartney, her German Shepherd, yips and whines. Still, he calls several times each week, always after midnight with slurs of pleading punctuated by threats. When she puts her phone on mute at ten p.m., his texts bloom like algae. Each morning, his messages begin with "Let's meet" before they skid from sentimentality to rage.

One night, McCartney stiffens and growls. Her daughters, thirteen and ten, sit up from their books, alert and listening. She hears scraping from the bathroom and knows he's remembered the window with the warped frame that makes it impossible to lock. She taps 911, gestures the girls to her side, and leads them outside to her car. From the kitchen window, as she pulls away, he displays two middle fingers. She doesn't hear barking. She doesn't see a strange car parked along the street, so she drives only a few blocks before turning left and then u-turning before parking, headlights extinguished. When the police pass by within minutes, she tells the girls, "He won't even have time to steal anything. This one will cost him more than an overnight and a warning."

She calls 911 again. "We're safe," she says. "Thank you."

In a voice barely above a whisper, Renee, the older girl, says, "No, we're not." Darcy, the younger, stares straight ahead as if she expects her father to appear.

The First Time

The five women are teachers, the husbands five different things, the party DJ'd by the IPod of the hosts. Twice, he turns up the volume. Twice, a woman, not the homeowner, turns it down. The third time, he dials the volume to jackhammer, and that woman's husband turns it off, the party on pause. He finishes his drink while she apologizes to everyone. He hears her repeat it as she asks for their coats. "It's not your house," she says when they are outside.

"Really? Like I don't know that? You act like I'm six."

"Not six. Drunk."

"You know what? You're a sponge. You suck all the joy out of the room, you and all the rest of those lightweights. That wasn't a party. That was a PTA meeting."

"Some of those lightweights have children waiting for them at home. They have baby sitters they have to drive home. Adult things."

"We don't have kids."

"Yes, we do. And a babysitter, too."

"We have a fucking sponge is what we have. This adult can drive it home."

"Not hardly," she says, showing him the keys.

For six miles, he is quiet. For a full day, she does not speak. "I'm supposed to say I'm sorry, right?" he finally says. "Ok, I'm sorry. Happy?"

She stares. "No, I'm not happy. Are you?"

"It's not like I touched you. It was just words."

"That's not an excuse, that's a deflection. If you ever touched me, it would be over."

New Year's Eve, Los Angeles

At 7:30, after taking Darcy to her friend's sleepover nine blocks away, she and Renee walk home together. Nearly there, they see an empty car double-parked, the driver's side door open, its lights extinguished. Here, after dark, fifty yards from home, their street always feels dangerous, alley-like, badly lit. Budget apartments sit below on one side instead of single-dwelling houses and duplexes like the ones set into the hillside on the other. She notices Renee veer right, and she drifts her way as subtly as she can muster. The next bend takes them into the street's deepest shadows just before the flight of stairs to their door.

"Those apartments are sketchy," Renee says, after they are inside and McCartney welcomes them. In the bedroom Renee and Darcy share, Renee chooses a record her grandfather has sent her for Christmas, one of the eight used albums of his he's guessed she'd love--Queen, Judy Collins, Linda Ronstadt, Harry Nilsson. She plays an entire side of Nilsson Schmilsson, singing softly along. The dog, instead of settling, is restless, pacing to windows. He doesn't bark.

An hour of music, and then she and Renee begin a second trip—another sleepover, the girls three years older for New Year's Eve five blocks away. As soon as they walk around the bend, they see two police cars by the double-parked car, its door still open, but now a girl is inside. Except for the policeman who waves to invite them past, whoever arrived in those two marked cars must be inside the apartments. "What you looking at, little bitch?" the girl says. The policeman's wave shifts into demand. "That's it, keep walking, little bitch," the girl calls as they pass him. "Fuck you, little bitch," she yells as they clear the scene.

"I wish I hadn't looked," Renee says when the street turns wider on the next block. "Did you look, Mom?"

"Yes."

"But she only talked to me."

"You're nearly as tall as I am already. You'll never see her again."

They have only three more blocks, both on the other side of an avenue where traffic is constant. They stand at the intersection, three streets intersecting the main highway, a series of left turn lights extending the wait. Down the sidewalk on their side, they see a small crowd has gathered where the apartments have a lower entrance.

"McCartney knew, didn't he?" Renee says, after they cross.

"Yes, he must have sensed when the police arrived."

The new year is less than three hours away when they reach the sleepover house. Both of her daughters will stay up for the bells and sirens and fireworks from thousands of yards spreading toward the city. "What do you think she could have done?" Renee says. "She didn't look much older than I am," whispering as if it were a secret.

Pentecostal

McCartney becomes a nuisance for unwelcome sounds. Car door slams. Voices passing on the street below. The wind driving a deck chair against the sliding, glass door. But he is security for the threats she does not hear. She reinforces McCartney with a motion sensor. Though coyotes, some nights, rouse the dog to barking before frightening her floodlight to brilliance. Renee and Darcy mostly seem to sleep through her double alarm. After a while, the coyotes, as if they have memorized where light begins, pace at the edge of darkness while McCartney does his extended solo.

One night, long after the coyotes have retreated, McCartney is so dissatisfied, she leashes him and steps outside. Across the highway and from beyond the hillside houses that end in wilderness, the glow of the latest wildfire has lengthened the radio's menu of languages. Fuego salvaje. Chay rung. Incendios. Smoke has drifted into the neighborhood. Evacuation is unlikely, but possible.

The vacant lot next door has been cleared of brush and damaged trees to lessen the chance of attracting embers. As if emptied, every nearby house is darkened, the ordinary and the reasonable already elsewhere or at rest. Although she sees that it's him at the edge of the light, McCartney is a lunge of howls.

The spotlight scorches them. He has something in his hands that looks like an axe handle or baseball bat. "I'll kill that dog if you let him go," he says. The girls, holding hands, appear behind her but do not speak. He crouches like a gargoyle, four steps, then three, close enough that she sees what he is carrying is the bottom half of his cue stick, what he hefts slowly from left to right and back again. "McCartney will hurt you first," she says. Renee begins to scream. He backs away and disappears.

Darcy says, "Why did McCartney bark at Dad this time?"

"McCartney's not stupid," Renee says. "He knows Dad is dangerous now."

From somewhere close, a car alarm begins to moan inside a garage like a steady pulse. From house to house, barking has erupted. Each flaring light translates their speeches, not into salvation, but, for now, reprieve.

Across Country

He sends a text to her about a shooting in the Pennsylvania town where they once lived. A jealous ex-husband has killed his former wife and her new boyfriend. At breakfast, Renee says, "Dad texted me a story from where we used to live. A shooting."

"Did you know those people?" Darcy says.

"No," she says at once. When she Googles the full story, she learns that the victims sat at an outdoor table so the shooter had no doors to open before and after he fired. A customer who conceal-carried burst through the restaurant's door and shot the killer twice. "A hero," one witness said, though both victims were dead and the killer managed to get back in his truck and drive away.

The girls have already read every word. "She wasn't doing anything wrong," Darcy says. "They hadn't been married for over a year."

"That restaurant wasn't there when I was growing up," she tells the girls. "I don't even know where it is." She does not tell them she went to high school with the woman who was killed. She says she didn't know either victim, which is true, at least, because she barely ever talked to that girl back then.

The Worst Time

"We're out of beer."

"You can't drive."

"I'm not drunk. It's three miles."

"You don't have a license." Remember why?"

"She's sleeping."

"Not for long."

"You think a few beers means I can't watch a sleeping baby?"

"And now she's awake."

He picked up the baby. "I'm carrying her. See? It's not hard."

"Put her down."

"I'll hold her until you come back. Fifteen minutes. Holding a baby isn't hard."

He walks with the crying baby to the balcony of their second-floor apartment. "Bring her back inside."

"You think I'll drop her?" He extends his arms over the railing. Darcy kicks at the air.

Now she is crying too. "My God. Please."

When he pulls her in and turns, she rushes at him and takes Darcy from his hands. He doesn't resist. "You're so OCD. I never knew that until this second one. You act like you never had a baby before, like Renee never happened and you're starting over." He opens the refrigerator and pulls out the last beer as she leads Renee and carries Darcy to the car.

"Hi, there," he says, when she reappears the next afternoon. "Look, I cleaned up. I vacuumed and did the dishes," but she walks into the bedroom to gather things into an overnight bag. "Look, no beer in the fridge," he says, but she passes him without speaking.

He calls down from the balcony just before she slams the car door shut behind her. "Never again," he says, which he repeats when she returns in three days, which holds true for eleven days.

When Darcy is Five

The cookie in her daughter's self-illustrated book has long hair cut into bangs so much like hers she says, "The gingerbread man is a girl," but Darcy explains he is wearing a wig. Her cookie runs out the kitchen door and escapes to run and play, but on the last page, that gingerbread man is trapped inside the three-dimensional, pop-up mouth of a scarlet fox, the wig gone in the final picture, lost, perhaps, in the struggle, and when she asks why he is smiling as he's being swallowed, Darcy says, "Because he only has one face."

When Renee is Eight

She draws twelve pages about a princess who needs to be saved. The door to her re-brick tower is chained shut for a dozen sunny days, her hair tightly curled and long, but nowhere near what would welcome a prince to climb. One line per page, this princess sings an abridged "Over the Rainbow." Bluebirds dot every clear sky. Lemon drops sparkle, then fade, but as she finishes, the prince, arriving on horseback, applauds and stays mounted. The rest of the story, Renee whispers, is a secret-secret.

The Mermaid Cemetery

For her eleventh birthday, Darcy asks for a trip to the mermaid cemetery near the ocean. The cemetery is surrounded by a fence with an ornate gate that says, "Welcome to look, but not to touch." Someone tends these graves. Someone has carried kelp and seaweed to vases brimmed with water Darcy tests with her fingertips. Renee says, "Stop," but Darcy licks her fingers, tasting the salt. Renee opens the brochure and begins to read the captions under the photographs that describe the histories of the mermaids who are buried beneath them. The girls follow the mulch trail among headstones shaped like fish, becoming mourners. Aloud, they both wish themselves transformed, wanting to change in order to have bodies that can live in water, scales swallowing their skin until their legs fuse, light and land abandoned, so deep below the surface, they will be impossible enough to be worshipped.

On Location

Renee tells her Emma Stone played tennis for a *Battle of the Sexes* scene on a nearby Los Angeles court. "Down by the fountain," she says, meaning the Riverside courts. Meaning not too far. Renee has played three times and plans to use her fourteenth birthday money to buy a vintage outfit like the one Emma Stone wears in the movie. Renee wants to swing her racket like Emma Stone, who had never played before she'd taken the part, but she thinks it would be hard to play with a wooden racket, so strange and heavy, its sweet spot small.

She drives Renee to the Riverside courts. They stand where

Emma Stone pretended to be Billie Jean King winning a tournament in San Diego. Less than 100 yards away a row of power lines towers up from where they follow US 5 and the roar of traffic.

Renee asks her to watch *Battle of the Sexes* again. They sit side by side on the couch. Conce. At last, Renee says, "Look, there it is, right where we were standing," and they watch Emma Stone run across the court, swing her wooden racket, and deliver a winning forehand as Renee leans against her.

Art School

One late afternoon she waits until a student's father who is late picks up his daughter from her art school. Renee and Darcy, who do their homework every day in her school office, are impatient, already packed to leave. The downstairs doors are locked. When the pounding on the back door begins, Renee says, "It's Dad. He saw me at the window."

She cracks a window and says, "Don't make your daughters see you get arrested."

"I'm not doing anything," he says. "There's no law against talking to my wife and kids."

"It's only six o'clock and you're drunk."

"You don't know that."

"The girls won't be talking. None of us are coming out until the police arrive." She holds her phone to her ear so he can see.

"You bitch," he shouts. "Fuck you," he yells, slamming his shoulder into the door. When it holds, he says, "You cunt" and walks away, but instead of leaving, he climbs the set of stairs to the parking lot and opens a car door.

Despite her warning, the girls are at the window now. "Whose car is that?" Renee says. "Why does he have a car?" He raises one arm and points something dark at the window where they stand. She is mesmerized, but Darcy drops and rolls into the office, Renee drops to her knees and follows her sister by crawling. Once they are inside, she runs into the office, locks the door, and taps 911.

"We do that drill in school," Darcy says.

"That's for elementary," Renee says. "Nobody in middle school will roll on the floor except weird kids. You'll see next year."

In less than a minute, a police helicopter hovers overhead, but by the time the police arrive by car, he is gone. There are security cameras outside the building and above the parking lot. "We need to confirm it was a gun," a policeman says.

"We're not crazy," she says. "The girls have been drilled. They both dropped as soon as he raised his arm," but the police say they need to study the object in his hand.

"Maybe it's a phone. It would be hard to tell," one says. "We have the make and model of the car. We have the license plate. We'll get the video enhanced and call you in for confirming things."

Minutes later, in the car, Darcy says, "Daddy could have shot all of us."

Renee says, "He just wants to shoot Mom."

The following day, she returns to the church where her art school for children, four to fourteen, is housed. This week the mediums are water color and acrylic painting, projects arranged by age and experience. News has spread. There are queries about security. A mother mentions the homeless served lunch by the parish; a father asks who controls the weekly AA meeting held inside a downstairs room. Someone lingers to suggest she consider a location dedicated exclusively to art, testing, as he speaks, the strength of the studio door, the challenge of its lock. Nobody says a word about the disturbance.

The day after that, a policewoman pauses the video where he's inside the car, his arm extended. "It's a phone, not a gun," she says. "See there?" The girls crowd closer, but she stays distant as if the image could materialize in the room. As if the policewoman is wrong. "We understand your fear," the woman says. "It would have been impossible to tell in the moment. You could still press charges for the threatening gesture."

"Good news, then," she says.

"Pressing charges? Yes, you could call it that."

The Last Time

Because school has just started, her art classes as well, she and the girls don't fly to Pennsylvania for his father's funeral. Because he wants to hang out with old friends, he flies to Las Vegas instead of home. "I need a ride," he says on the phone.

"No," she says to herself. "Why?" she says aloud, and he short-lists, "You don't have school. Neither do the girls. It's not that far. My friends took off. My card is maxed out." As if Las Vegas is a field trip. As if it's about her guilt.

Darcy says, "How far is Las Vegas?" Renee says, "Why can't he ride the bus?" She says, "You'll see."

The trip takes nearly four hours. As he wheels his suitcase toward the car, she nods at the paper bag he carries. "It's barely noon," she says. "We have another four hours in front of us."

"It's not open," he says, something worse, because she can smell it on him before he displays the full bottle and unscrews the cap. He nurses the vodka for a few minutes before he asks her to stop at a KFC as they are leaving the city behind.

"Nobody else here eats that," she says.

"Is that right, girls? You don't want any extra crispy?"

Renee grips Darcy's arm to remind her not to answer. He comes back to the car with a bucket. "Did you at least bring napkins?" she says. He settles in on a drumstick.

An hour later, she and the girls have to pee. When he lifts the bottle in salute, she sees it is nearly empty. They are gathering a few snacks in the convenience store when Darcy looks out the glass door and shouts, "Daddy's sick." He's sprawled on the sidewalk; Renee begins to cry. Outside, they both hold back while she shakes him, but he doesn't respond.

"Your husband?" the store manager says from the doorway. "I've already called. I can't have that here."

"The police?"

"He doesn't need a cop. He needs a doctor."

Even with the windows down, the car is torrid in mid-afternoon. She sends the girls back into the store. Customers turn their heads as they pass. Some loiter by the large front window. On their way out, they look in another direction. Before long, the EMTs start an IV and load him into the ambulance. She tells Renee to dump the rest of the chicken and the empty bottle into the trash can that stands just outside the entrance. "Where are you taking him?" she asks the driver.

"Las Vegas," he says.

"We're on our way back to Los Angeles. That's like starting over."

"There's no help between here and there," he says. "You must know that from being on this road before." There is nothing to do but follow. In the hospital cafeteria, while he is "under observation," their early dinners are so bland, they are hard to swallow.

Near twilight, he is wheeled to their car. "It was so fucking hot sitting in the car while you were pissing. I got myself out, but the fucking parking lot gave me a knockout punch." She stares straight ahead and drives. In the back seat, the girls pretend they can still see to read. After it is full dark, he says, "Route 66 is out here, girls. Where everything was cool once." Nobody speaks. "You're right, girls. There's nothing to even see here. No wonder nobody lives here. Fucking desert. It just puts you to sleep." A few houses blink by at a crossroad. "Somebody's awake there, but not for long, I bet. Nobody sleeps In Las Vegas because it's cool inside and the lights stay on. If we were there, we'd all be awake and talking where they know how to live in the desert without boring people into a coma."

As they pass into the city, he says, "So, nobody's talking?"

Rollover

In the third year of drought, her house foreshadows ashes. For several days, the texts and phone calls cease, but then a police woman calls. "From the art school dust-up," she says. "I recognized your ex's name at the scene. I thought I could give you a head's up."

"Your father was in an accident," she tells the girls. "In that car we saw at the art school, with the woman who owns it."

"A bad accident?" Renee says.

"A rollover. The car's a loss."

"Is he dead?" Darcy says.

"No. He was driving. The passenger side door took the full force of a large tree."

"She's dead?" Renee says and begins to cry.

"Not yet."

"Was he drunk?" Darcy says. "Did he fall asleep like that time in the desert?"

"Yes, and maybe."

"So, he goes to jail?" Renee says.

"Probably."

"I hate that word," Renee says. "That and *maybe* and *hopefully*."

"And 'we'll see'," Darcy says. "Like we can't see anything right now. Like we're blind."

"Like we won't know what's happening until it's over," Renee says. "Right, Mom?"

The Past Tense of the Census

In the national census year, before they moved to Los Angeles, she had sought part-time work, self-designed hours convincing her to canvas the county of farms and quiet, well-zoned streets. There were heads to count, assessment questions, and not every house, she soon learned, was welcoming. House trailers were rare and always alone, set so often on barely landscaped lots that she was surprised by one site's borders of high wooden fence, a lawn weed-infested, yet closely mown by somebody, she thought, who was taking whatever care he could, not a man who, before she reached the door, opened it and stood naked, except for sandals, two steps above her.

Once exposed, she thought, a man might be capable of anything. She backed away, saying nothing, fishing for her keys. She kept her eyes on him, but he didn't move. She drove back to the house they rented where he was babysitting, four weeks out of rehab and two months sober. Darcy and Renee, three and nearly six, skittered around the fenced-in back yard. Twilight settled in. They stood beside the deck rail so the girls could see they were watching. Their neighbor's Black Lab barked longingly at its fence gate as she began, hushed and intimate, to speak.

Was that guy drunk? he asked. *I don't think so.* What did he say? *He was soundless.* What did he do? *He showed himself.* How close was he? *Pounce distance.* And right there her story ended as if she was willing to tear only one page from her notebook of memory. By then, all she could make out of their daughters was movement. "They're getting hard to see," she said.

"Just wait," he said. "In a little while, they'll disappear."

III

Stunned

Sometimes, he has learned, the eyes of birds weigh more than their brains. Sometimes their bones weigh less than their feathers. Sometimes, while touching her face, he became a boy excited when her eyes exclaimed, "Yes, go on." Sometimes, undressed, she felt weightless when her body lifted toward him.

None of that extraordinary as the moment she became an etched inscription on a plaque—She Loved, She Would Have, She Was—an odd conjugation of loss, a wound placed within the private museum of his past where light was absorbed after her flight was interrupted by the levitation of accident.

WAIL

Dale's dog, an Eskimo Spitz named Blizzard, had thrown up three times the night before and had diarrhea during the day. "Maybe she'll pull out of it," he told his wife.

"You hoped for too long," Cilla said.

When Blizzard began to whimper and cry, Dale thought the dog sounded just like Cilla, who, in her nightmares, made a whining sound that extended into a wail that raised goose-flesh on his body. Something about that sound—its pitch set exactly to terror—made Dale lie in the dark and listen, trying to somehow eavesdrop on the scene that was causing her distress.

He'd never learned what was happening in her dreams. That wail never turned into a scream. He'd never touched or shaken her awake, and she had never woken or remembered what she had dreamed.

And now, he didn't argue with Cilla, wishing he had called yesterday or even the day before, especially since the vet's hours had ended while Dale was taking care of Blizzard's latest mess. The office didn't open again until eight a.m.

Because the forecast was for a perfect, late-spring evening, Dale carried the dog outside and laid her as gingerly as he could on an old bed spread under the backyard weeping cherry. Though he knew she could barely stand, he tied the leash around the trunk and clipped it to Blizzard's collar before he said "Goodnight," and went inside.

Just after midnight, Blizzard began to wail. Each time she quieted, Dale held his breath and hoped, but soon she began again, extending the terrible, pain-infused cry. When Dale opened the back door as it first grew light, the dog was unable to rise to her feet. He laid a bowl of water beside her and sat on the damp grass, but Blizzard began to wail again, making the sound of hopelessness.

On the deck next door, his neighbors, an elderly couple, were out early to sit with coffee. Dale held his breath, afraid they would shout accusations. Maybe they had even called the police, Dale thought, and he carried Blizzard to the car inside the blanket, carefully circling his house on the side opposite where his neighbors were perched.

He drove for over an hour, the radio turned down to a murmur for the first few miles, then switched off. Blizzard, at last, drifted off with the motion. Just before eight, he arrived at the vet's. When Dale slowed and parked, Blizzard whimpered, but she lay quietly on the blanket as he carried her to the front door.

Another car was parked farther away, but now the driver's side door opened and a woman swung her legs out to allow a small, lively leashed terrier to scramble past her. "My God," she said. "Whatever have you there?"

Dale turned to face the door. He heard the woman's footsteps on the gravel. The terrier yipped twice. As soon as the attendant unlocked the door, Dale stepped past him. He kept his eyes on the receptionist, softly starting an apology, not looking back at the attendant or the woman with the dog as Blizzard, without lifting her head or stirring, began to whine, the pitch unchanged, not extending into wail, but into silence.

SUMMITING

Not exactly Mt. Everest, but we don't have $100,000+ to spend, what some people call a bargain because summiting there is "singular" and loaded with "bragging rights." Trust me, this one is semi-famous, snow-capped, at least, in July, and, for sure, we're waiting in line to summit just like the Everest elitists when a wealthy mountaineer panics at one of the dangerous parts. Maybe you've seen that video, some goggle-wearing adventure-seeker stuffed into a bulky out-fit balking at a reach-and-swing-and-hold-or-else-die-mo-ments. A Sherpa coaxing. Fear forever documented. My wife keeps saying not to sound sour-grapy, (she calls it heartless) but I plan to post a video from my body-cam to prove we never hesitated while climbing a risky patch.

Right now, the camera is off because there's nothing to cor-roborate but other summiteers here where breath comes hard and discomfort easy. My wife, the bean-counter, says there are 68 in front of us, and I know not to challenge. Spend-ing less, we expected to wait, but our foot traffic is clogged like Black Friday at the Miracle Mile Mall the year we were married.

Ruby anniversary, I told my wife; let's not wait for gold to try our luck with peril. Let's do something so it's memorable for more than the year or two we might have left after our fiftieth. We even trained for a few days, paying a mentor, a group lesson, economy package. Another couple, both look-ing decrepit, shared how excited they were to learn we were ruby-marrieds, too. Maybe they found each other late, I said, meaning a decade, easy.

If our actuarial tables are right, we'll have thirteen years, give or take some, to always remember overcoming the advertised hazards. My wife, the spoilsport, says she'll never forget the money that went to gear, guide, and travel that's gift-wrapped discomfort and impatience while we wait for our few thousand dollars-worth of terror.

What else I'll remember is that when some big mouth standing close to us declared we're safer here than we will be driving home, I had to raise that bar by pointing out our home is a seven-hour drive, the back half through landscape where water and rescue are in short supply. When only shrugs followed that logic, I turned inward, concentrating on freezing in July, my wife in purple, me in green, what she chose for us at Summit Outfitters, that word so versatile it's an adjective, too.

Admittedly, things have soured. Even though we left Summiting Lodge at 5 AM today, hoping to beat the rush, here we are stalled at 8 AM surrounded by adventurers who probably thought the same way as us about anniversaries and birthdays and retirement presents, pre-paying for photographs and a certificate of achievement to frame. For sure, we're all co-signers of a detailed waiver.

"Don't you fret. Today's window is open wide," our group-guide calls in a voice that suggests he might do a bit of yodeling on the peak, but anyone can see that the sun is safely above the horizon, nothing above us but blue sky and dozens of climbers and guides snaking up "Summit Leg." Not much different than a backup on the first tee of my often-wind-swept golf course because of a surprise overnight freeze.

Before we start moving, let me tell you a story. Last night, at dinner, I gave my wife a gag gift, an authentic replica of special summiting insurance, the kind that promises transportation of our bodies if we fall down a cliff or into an altitude-induced coma, the one that guarantees a thorough search for our bodies. She didn't laugh or smile. She was icy. She folded it into her purse for what she said was "safekeeping."

Listen, I'm telling you that because I have to admit sorrow appears to have settled upon my wife as if this thrill, too, has gone the way BB King once warned us. "Orgasmic," the guide said when we took our place in line a few hours ago, grinning at my wife as if suggesting she hasn't enjoyed that in quite some time. He leered at me, too, maybe making sure he was being inclusive.

It was too late to fire him, but I vowed not to tip afterward. After all, forty years is a summit, too, something we'd been standing on since midnight, though it seems, as my wife, the mountaineer, trudges, head-down, ahead of me, my body-cam recording nothing but her bent, but dogged posture, a steep and slippery metaphor.

The Look-Alike Doll

After her mother selects the photo meant to become her doll's face, the girl is overjoyed to play with her infant self. She gazes at that familiar baby, mothering its small, resilient body. But when she sleeps with herself, she dreams of shrinking. Anxious, she takes photos of herself and searches for one that will fit the body she is terrified to lose. When nothing matches, she crawls inside the closet where everything too small to wear is stored. She whimpers with her forgotten voice, stuffs two fingers into her mouth, and sucks on those toys to keep from screaming.

IQ TEST

My mother said she had seen a photograph of a child prodigy's parents posed beside him as part of the good news feature of the seven o'clock news. "He's only twelve," she said, "and he's entering medical school and puberty at the same time, isn't that something? By the time he's your age, he'll be a surgeon, somebody able to have my life in his hands."

My mother loved stories about boy-geniuses. Since I'd started first grade, my future was supposed to wear scrubs, wash its hands in scalding water, and answer a body's questions with skillfully-handled blades, but I was already nineteen, too old for any description with the prefix "boy." For a while, as she went on about the child-doctor, I watched her preparing tomatoes for canning. Then, she asked the question she'd been holding inside all summer. "How's my doctor coming along?"

Steam rose toward the kitchen ceiling like expectations. When I didn't answer right away, she said she'd heard somewhere that the brightest people have the earliest memories. "I bet that boy remembers wearing diapers," she said. "What do you remember?"

That was a question I knew the answer to. "My head being shaved because of the ringworm you said I caught at the barbershop. Then everybody calling me 'baldy.'"

"That's when you were four," my mother said, sounding disappointed. "How about something from when you were three?"

I decided to go with something else from when I was four that must have happened earlier. "The day I started wearing those steel-braced shoes because I walked funny."

"See?" she said. "You were three years and seven months to the day. By then, everybody knew you were smart." She looked at the clock that hung on the wall above the kitchen sink as if she was about to announce the exact minute those braces and been set in place, but then she turned and sighed so heavily I knew what was behind all this were my recent grades. "They're less than perfect," was how she had put it when they'd arrived. As if she was uneasy mentioning the letter C or, I was sure, not daring to say D aloud because it was blasphemy. "Try to remember your toddler year," she finally said. Which I took for the pre-brace year, and what I remembered was nothing whatsoever, as empty of answers as I'd been for the final exam in organic chemistry.

"The super snow drifts," I said, beginning with something safe while my mother leaned back into those tomatoes, taking a stab at the winter of '77 when we still lived near Buffalo. I'd heard about that blizzard every late January when the anniversary of "the big one" rolled around. "There was one so high somebody stood on it and touched a live wire."

My mother started humming, and I coasted into the summer before. "Dad, in the new, used GTO, singing "Afternoon Delight" while we drove to Niagara Falls."

"Yes!" my mother nearly screamed. "Yes, he about ruined that trip with all that talk about 'skyrockets in flight.'"

"And Barry Manilow," I said, figuring there must have been a hit that summer for my mother's favorite singer.

"'I Write the Songs,'" she said, and sang a few lines. "That's my boy," she said. "That's my brain surgeon coming back to life."

I kept on spellbinding her with my high IQ of nostalgia, but I didn't say a word about having already changed my ma jor from pre-med to history. I loved following all those time-lines that detailed how everything and everywhere and everybody became the way we were. If my mother asked when she finally found out, I'd start by saying they were like arteries and veins and capillaries, an enormous circulatory system.

I boarded the express trance through my year number one and rode it all the way back to my birth. I'd seen enough photographs to describe my mother's hair, how it was curled, held tight to her scalp with pastel pins. I knew the nurse would be saying "it's a boy," that mystery still solved on the spot in 1974. I felt the doctor's gloved hands on my emerging head, heard the nurse saying "one last push," giving that first day everything it needed to certify me as absolutely brilliant until, seeing her beaming beside a winter's worth of tomatoes in perfectly sealed jars, I vanished myself back into the sea of darkness inside her, sucking my thumb and kicking, then passing beyond gender and the wiring up of the brain, whatever insisted my genius was true until I became just words my mother murmured to my father as he touched her or said to herself before she even knew him.

KAFKAESQUE

Sleep, as always, came reluctantly. An hour of changing positions from one discomfort to another. Often, several minutes of an imagined crisis in his heart or his lungs or some unidentifiable, essential organ. Eventually, an urgent bathroom trip. A short stint of depressurizing by sitting up in a living room chair. Pacing to unravel his tension. Counting steps to 1000 before deciding that round number must be a lullaby. Fitful, he props two pillows, lies on his back, and at last, during his very early morning exhaustion sleep, still restless, the dream.

His friend and colleague is babbling nonsense in a long hall of many doors, unaware of the spectacle he's making. The students, only a very few because it is early, pass by without comment like well-rehearsed extras. Though his colleague will not stop his garbled chattering, he recognizes a second professor staring from a doorway. He notices another observing from farther up the hall. As if they are props, they are both stationary, but now he hears himself speaking clearly. "Let's find your office and wait for this to pass," he says, nodding to guide his incoherent friend. "I'll stay with you until you can say my name."

He keeps on spewing advice until his friend goes silent. As he says, "There, that's better," his friend points at him, and he realizes, looking down, that his shoes, though both neatly tied, are mismatched. What's more, the rest of his body is naked, and he now remembers walking unclothed across the campus, passing a few dozen students who either did not see him or did not care, even when he stopped at the cafeteria for the cinnamon bun and coffee he is still holding. He grips the paper cup tightly and squeezes the sweet roll, his hands so busy there is no way to cover himself.

His friend, at least, remains calm, his talkative lapse passed, and they begin to walk. Where is his friend's office? For that matter, where is his own? They pass door after door. Ahead of them, a small gathering of students who must see a calm, well-dressed professor and a naked one. He tries a locked door and then another and wakes, terrified in a new, unsettling way--not screaming or even panting into hyperventilation. His heart rate steady and unhurried as if he's sedated. As if that scene was from the very recent past.

The clock reads 4:46, late summer, no longer the half-light of a month ago, and though he cannot bear to lie in bed, he cannot make himself stand. What's more, no matter what he tells himself, he does not even move. Surely, his head will clear. Isn't that the advice he had given to his disoriented friend, a man not much older than he is? "You just need to get your feet under you," he had said. "Find a familiar place. Get settled in your office. The comfort of your own chair. Things that will help you focus."

All of his phrases had echoed: Everything will be ok in a little while. Take a few minutes. They'll do you good. You'll see. Trust me.

Time, as well, had turned staccato: Exceedingly soon. A breath away. A heartbeat. A wish.

The Au Pair

In early June, a week after our neighbor's husband left for somewhere he didn't care to reveal, a young man cut her lawn. The next afternoon, he trimmed the shrubbery that surrounded her house. He looked about as old as our grandson Jack, who was about to graduate from college.

By the following day, he was out walking her dog and retrieving her mail. His car, my husband pointed out, had been in the driveway overnight. "That boy has moved in," he said. I couldn't disagree.

My husband, always the green thumb, saw fit to get himself busy where our yards segue into each other, but whoever it was didn't come out for more yard work despite what my husband pointed out was a whole day's worth of weeding that needed to be done over there. I didn't argue. I baked two loaves of banana bread and carried one to the neighbor's front door. I bartered bread for news.

"She called him her au pair," I said, as soon as I shut our kitchen door behind me. "Lawrence, she said his name was. She accented the second syllable so it came out 'Le-Ronce'."

"Au pair?" he said, as if trying to remember something from high school French or a movie with subtitles. "She's paying him to live there?"

"Room and board is the standard," I said, as if 'au pair' was advertised frequently in our local weekly newspaper.

"That's a thing?" he said. "If that's the case, our daughter could have saved herself a bundle if Jack had found a woman in need to live with instead of wasting her money in that expensive dorm,"

He ranted like that off and on about "the arrangement" for a few weeks, but I got the gist of the legitimate side of it. The au pair babysat. The mother worked. There were reasons it made sense, though after a while my husband's qualms, at least the public ones, seemed to be grounded in truth. The yard was taking a turn for the worse. Lawrence didn't edge like our neighbor's lost husband. Worse, he was doing a sketchy job with the weeds. There were swings in the yard but neither of the kids came outside. They seemed to have become indoor pets.

"Those kids are old enough to walk a dog and not wander off," my husband reminded me from time to time. "They can make a sandwich and remember to close the refrigerator." Those children, I admitted, were getting up there, one going into the middle school, one not much younger, but I did some homework on 'au pair' before I brought up a solution. "She could be serious about him tutoring the kids," I said. "Maybe it's no accident they're not getting much of a summer vacation."

"I bet she is. They're getting some supplementary education over there."

"Or maybe a crash course in French," I said, remembering the accent.

"French? I won't even say what I'm thinking now. LeRonce is nothing but a Larry, you can put your money on that."

By August, I had to admit that some sort of vine was creeping over half of the shrubbery. The au pair, who at least still cut the grass, didn't seem to notice. Thistle and some other noxious weeds my husband gave names to sprouted between the bushes. After a while, they towered in menacing way. The house itself looked shabbier, as if it had turned sorrowful.

"By now, those kids must be speaking French like natives," my husband said, not in a friendly way. When school began, the au pair's car didn't move for weeks. As if it were waiting for AAA to show up, it stayed in the driveway a few feet from where the kids waited for the bus each morning. Deliveries arrived from the grocery store, the pharmacy, and Amazon. "I guess Larry dropped out of college," my husband said.

In October, we saw the au pair rake leaves for half an hour, making four small, colorful piles that blew apart and scattered before dark. The vines and weeds, still untouched, went dormant. After Halloween, we never again saw him outside. "Home improvements," I said. "There's plenty to do around the house to earn your keep."

"Tas de merde," he said, proud of himself for Googling how to swear in French.

"You mispronounced that," I said.

"Garce," he mumbled.

"That one, too."

But now, our neighbor didn't leave her house. "Maybe she's working from home, too," I speculated, and my husband said, "Get real" in English.

The boy shoveled the first heavy snow in December. He wheeled the garbage can to the sidewalk. "He's alive, at least," my husband said, laughing a little, and I gave him my schoolmarm stare.

And then, as the year expired, the au pair's car disappeared and so, we concluded, had he. "Maybe his Visa expired," my husband said.

"You're not funny," I said.

I didn't tell him that I felt sad that the au pair had left. Since way back in August, I'd envied our neighbor. While my husband pointed out the poor yard work, I started thinking of the difference between a yard well-tended and a body coaxed to pleasure. I wanted our weeds to flourish. I wished for all of our shrubs to be left unpruned, growing as ragged and wild as the innuendoes of neglect. I wanted a vine to embrace them and never let go.

THE YEAR OF EXTRAVAGANT ADDITIONS

Roy Keller's family had his basement redone, creating what his father called a den. It had a mahogany bar, shelves for dozens of bottles, and hooks where all sizes of glasses hung like sparkling hats. My father didn't drink.

Chris Coleman's family had an in-ground swimming pool overlooked, on one side, by a redwood deck that was screened to keep out bugs. My father couldn't swim.

My father loved music, but all his records were 78's, even in 1958, so I had to buy plastic inserts for my 45's and play them one at a time. But never when he was sleeping after his night shift and never loudly when he was awake.

However, my best friend was Jack Stankowski, and his family had a Living Garage, a room his father had added to their house where he could park his Cadillac. "The Caddie's in our house," Jack said. "For real," he added, as if the room would vanish, and I had to agree because the only thing separating that car from where we were sitting in his living room was a nearly wall-to-wall double-glass panel that slid open and shut. From our overstuffed pale blue chairs, we could see the Cadillac sitting there like a huge indoor pet. My father drove home from work in a four-year-old Chevy five days a week and parked it in the street.

Jack knew all about the Living Garage. His father subscribed to Esquire, where there was a full-color ad with a picture of what Jack said was a Lincoln, the colors labeled Starmist White over Flamingo. "Bring luxury inside," the ad said, and Jack's father had listened. Jack cleaned up after that car, erasing, with dry mop, its tracks from the red tile swirled with white like marbling in expensive steak. He dusted the chrome, even calling that Cadillac "Alexander" as if it might follow him to the kitchen to beg for food.

Maybe I imagined it, but even if the garage was empty when we watched television in Jack's living room, I thought I could smell a faint trace of exhaust, as if we were sitting in a tunnel. And for sure, I was always surprised when the Cadillac reappeared, Jack's father pulling up tight to the back wall, the glow from the headlights pinching small on the rustic paneling like pupils on a sunny beach. When Jack's father emerged, his suit looked like one worn by a corporate lawyer from a distant planet where cars had souls. He always locked the sliding glass before he nodded our way and walked past us, turning ordinary as he vanished through the hallway door.

That Cadillac had an extravagant sound system. When Jack's parents went out for the night in bad weather, they used their Buick, and we turned up the radio and listened, hoping to hear our favorite songs surround us. "Only five," Jack would say, afraid of running the car battery down. "Only five," even if we'd heard Frank Sinatra and Brenda Lee and Connie Francis, wasting most of our Cadillac time before going inside for television.

It was hard, but Jack kept to that limit until one rainy night when Jack used his father's spare key to turn the engine over when the DJ, before what would have been the fifth song, announced he was about to spin a Triple Play of Chuck Berry. "Nobody's coming home for an hour yet," he said. "Let's listen like we're cruising."

"We should open the garage door," I said after "Sweet Little Sixteen" ended. "People kill themselves like this."

"If we open the door, my dad kills us when somebody tells him the Caddie's been running in the garage. We haven't even been in here ten minutes. Nobody dies that fast."

The DJ read two commercials before he said, "Come on, turn it up," and the Del Vikings started singing "Come Go with Me." We slapped the dashboard, mouthing the "Dumdums," but after it ended and the DJ broke in with another ad, I had a better reason to stop besides the headache I had. "Your Mom and Dad will smell the fumes when they get home."

"Okay," Jack said, but then "Young Blood" by the Coasters came on and he turned up the volume another notch.

Nosed between the towering cactus and the rubber plant that Jack's mother had placed in two corners to help make it more living room than garage, the Caddie, by the time the Coasters were finished, seemed to be driving on a line between the Sahara and the jungle. The DJ said, "Here's Elvis," his voice sounding distant, but the song was "Loving You," not the flip side "Teddy Bear" that we loved, and Jack turned off the engine. "I do feel a little sick," he said.

Jack opened the garage door then. It had stopped raining, and we stood where the tile, right before it ended where the driveway began, was still dry under the overhang, both of us breathing deep. Jack didn't say a word, but I was thinking we'd been saved because the DJ had played a slow song. If he'd played "Teddy Bear," we would have listened. If he'd followed that with anything at all by Little Richard, we would have sat there happy, falling asleep just before the news came on.

After Six Years, the News

When Harry arrives, his mother tells him a peacock has blown into her neighborhood, driven from Griffith Park by a record, Pacific wind. Lucky, she says, we have all these trees. From outside there is a loud squawk that sounds close.

"Mmwaah-ah." The peacock, Harry thinks. "Mmwaah-ah" the second call lifting at the end like a question, louder and foreign. Tropical, he thinks, nearly threatening. "Listen to that, Harry," his mother says. "Sue Ellen named it Dorothy."

"It's female?"

"I was going to look it up but haven't gotten around to it. Anyway, it's more fun to believe it's a girl swept here like little Judy Garland."

"Mmwaah-ah." The third call resonates so close Harry says, "Let's go outside and take a look."

"Oh, that's not Dorothy," his mother says. "That's Sue Ellen. She's gotten really good at imitating the call, but I can tell the difference. She saw your car and is showing off."

The next call, from near the front door, seems, to Harry, a sound-check for lunacy. "How often does she do that?" he says, whispering in spite of himself, but his mother is already hurrying to the door.

Sue Ellen is enormous, wrapped in so much olive-shaded loose cloth that Harry thinks she might be wearing a makeshift sari to pique the peacock's curiosity. She looks Harry up and down and says, "The prodigal son. Aren't you the lucky one to be welcomed back."

"I'm not making him any feast," his mother says. "But this

is my second day of fasting, so there's plenty in the refrigera=
tor he can help finish."

"Fasting?" Harry says. His mother has always been what
everyone calls "petite."

"Three days every month. There's proof it makes you live
longer."

Sue Ellen pats her stomach. "I never miss a meal, and here
I am seventy-seven like that place on Sunset Strip way back
when your mother was a twinkle in your grandfather's eye."

Harry's mother has told him that Sue Ellen has run
through three husbands, and he reconsiders her size, the sort
of men who would have loved unwrapping her. "Your Mom
told you about Dorothy, right? That beauty was up on my
roof this morning. She's too smart for coyotes. She loves be=
ing up there on the red tiles with that great view. If she could
work a camera, she could take pretty pictures of Los Angeles
from up there."

"The peacock made the news," Harry's mother says, lift=
ing the newspaper, already folded to a photograph, from her
coffee table. "See there? That's Sue Ellen's roof and there's
Dorothy."

"They didn't bother to write anything about her," Sue Ellen
says. "All they put in was a caption as if something like this
happened every day. Like it's not a story."

"They should have printed it in color," Harry says, but nei=
ther woman smiles.

Sue Ellen gathers her off-green drapery around her. "Pea=
cocks don't need a color photograph. Everybody knows how
beautiful they are. Wait until you see how deep the blue is on
Dorothy's neck."

Harry thinks a deep blue neck means the bird is male, but he lets it pass. "I'll leave you two lovebirds alone to catch up," Sue Ellen says. "I just wanted to take a look at Junior."

Sue Ellen gone, Harry's mother sets five plastic containers on the kitchen table. "Take your pick," she says. "It's hard when you're fasting and have a fridge full of leftovers. I can't keep any of this for another two days." As he opens each one, her head snaps from side to side like a bird's, making Harry afraid she's begun rehearsing peacock mannerisms in order to keep up with Sue Ellen's vocals.

Mmwaah-ah—the sound renews itself like an argument. "It's uncanny how good Sue Ellen is, isn't it?" his mother said. "They say peacocks talk more when they're mating."

Mmwaah-ah. Nearly a honk, Harry thinks. He has to admit that Sue Ellen emits the same sound each time, but either the peacock isn't fooled or else it senses the need for silence. "Maybe so," he says, "but her version sounds lonely."

His mother, sixteen years on her own and six without a visit from him, goes quiet. When the calls pause, all that arrives is traffic noise from the highway two streets below, a furious surge that announces the stoplight has changed. She sighs heavily when he says, "No thanks" to the leftovers.

"The doctor says the horse is out of the barn about what's going on with me," she says, "but there's no harm in trying things. Starve the good part of yourself, starve the bad, too, right?" She closes each lid. "Let's go look out back while there's still good light."

As soon as they're on the patio, his mother calls, "Mmwaah-ah." Her bleat doesn't sound anything like a peacock, but Harry smiles and wraps his arms around her. "It sounds silly when I try," she says. "Like I'm either stupid or dying."

"You'll be fine, Mom. Just different. Short, skinny women live practically forever."

"Or six years?" she says. "Maybe long enough to last until your next visit." He waits for her to push off, but she doesn't pull away. He thinks he sees color and movement over her shoulder, but he wants to be sure before he slowly turns her.

Lazarus in the Forest

In the bathtub, alone, he lies face down and counts in the shallow water. In the neighbor's bright yellow plastic swimming pool, he stares up at the rippling sky as the girl who lives there counts. At night, he holds a pillow over his face to become a fourth-grade victim until his mother, in the doorway, says, "You're asking for big trouble."

Instead, he shifts to pressing the pillow in daylight, timing himself, checking the sweep hand of his Timex watch for how many seconds he can last before coming up gasping to check, sometimes extending his score like a record setter for survival.

Kid stuff, his father says, when his mother catches him again. He'll get over it when he knows his limits. And soon, like the bathtub and the swimming pool, the pillow is left behind when he learns what the mystics do, shutting down the pulse with a block of wood under the armpit, pressure that produces a tourniquet effect.

He lays fingers to his wrist as he dies, then returns again and again to that brief sensation, dying in the basement or the garage, or better, among the trees in the game lands where he is never to be alone, lying down where someone might discover him.

He stares at the path he takes to a small clearing, imagining hikers being startled or anxious or afraid when they see how his body is so still. He wants someone to panic. He wants someone to cry or even scream. Lying there, sprawled like the drowned, he anticipates the power of leaving and returning. And when no one appears, he imagines the fingertips on his wrist or his throat. The CPR, his first great gasp that holds his rescuer in wonder when he is becomes the chosen who re-emerges, breathing like the singular.

AMONG THE SWINGS

The boy is the second teenager stuck in one of the park's baby swings this month, the first a fourteen-year-old girl who laughed when her friend filmed two firemen tugging until they finally soaped her free. The three of us became a home movie that has two million views, ninety per cent of them within the first forty-eight hours.

I'm here by myself this time. This boy is fourteen, too, thin and girlish. He giggled once before he caught something in my expression that shut him up, a silent wiggle-worm with ants in his pants, wearing the childish names my mother and her sisters all used on boys they thought were too squirrely for their own good. A boy, I learned early, not to be.

But when a crowd begins to gather, including boys his age with phones, he outgrows those names, the ones he's earning now unmentionable if you're being filmed like I am. Even if you're a volunteer. Because you live in this town and have a job in its high school and children of your own nearly that age.

I settle for "dork" and leave even that unspoken. Here he is, immovable, even his skinny ass outgrown this chair by six or seven years. His friends, I'd bet, tried squeezing into that swing, largest first, like some sort of Goldilocks variation, leaving him behind for the bears to deal with. By now, at least one of them, maybe all, are among them. Like arsonists gathering at the fire they set in an abandoned building.

I can take my time with this. He's not a cat in a tree, a little girl crying beneath it. There are no lives in danger here, just this kid playing the fool, an idiot, a jag off, that old standby from where I grew up, from when I was fourteen and called everyone that name until they labeled me in return.

I could cut the rubber and be done, but then there'd be the cost and time for replacement, maybe weeks, mid-summer, with one less swing for a four-year-old. I have the soap with me, but it can wait. He can't help trying one more time to free himself while I approach him, sure that every move is being recorded. But this is old news before it even happens, maybe a few thousand views, maybe less, maybe not even being posted because who cares about this twerp coming late to the party?

I wait a little longer. He tries again. When I move no closer, I sense phones being raised from so many angles that a few of them might get this right, a fresh take on an outdated story. Whether it's shame he feels when I don't touch him. Or anxiety. Or maybe fear this time as he wiggles and squirms himself into something so immature that the afternoon fills with enough brutal synonyms for childish and infantile that when I turn and walk away he will shrivel and shrink small enough to free himself without a hero to embrace and embellish him.

Apocalypse

The Event

The authorities are helpless. The scientists confused. Mixed messages come and go like the sun. No one has ever planned for widespread fire beneath the earth, how something so much like soil uses air to attack us. But now we see what 1000 degrees does, the hot spots we watch in the way we inspect our fireplaces for the unlucky ember before sleep. But now we live over exhaust, thirty-five parts per million on a monoxide alarm that sends a siren into our sleep. Our neighbors have boarded up hope; the government stands ready to raze the future of where we live, all that's left to us of politics. The earth, we have learned, is fuel. Beneath us is an eternal candle.

The Neighbors

We are three couples walking into a field plowed under to suppress the height of flares. A winter without snow squats over us and refuses to go. There is a kind of half-light we have grown used to, the cleared landscape draped at one end as if its window were ragged and broken. It takes miles of driving, now, before the sky can surprise us, but this night we stand together and scuff the soil, the moon seeming to search only for us like a weak-battery flashlight that can make nothing out for certain. Even if God held it, he would still need to call, "Is that you?" or "Who's there?" For a few minutes, the oldest of us works his shoes in the loose soil, shifting in tiny increments like a wrist wrestler trying to get a slim advantage of leverage. The nearest exhaust pipe is twenty yards away. Another one stands forty yards off. Those remnants of hope, like our town, have been abandoned for months. "Right now," he says, "we're the opposite of Noah, standing here on the first piece of the earth to die." His wife says, "For years, we have been sleeping with a leper without noticing our faces have disappeared." The rest of us nod to both. I imagine a toll gate, someone ringing a contagion bell to warn the foolish away from our small, but expanding country.

The Looters

They came to the empty houses in our town, each boarded and locked after our neighbors left for the last time, leaving behind the things they would live without. Backyard vents still shaped the world beneath us into columns of smoke that turned the looters wary and timid. When the last stand of nearby trees ignited, the looters fled in their half-filled trucks, driving the road-blocked highway where the earliest fissures yawned.

The News

We were the second town to be devastated. Because the world believed it was singular, the first was famous, periodically, for years. We were talked about for days. But after a fire, from underground, reached another town, the soap-smooth voices at press conferences washed themselves and left. After the closest forests to a third, fourth, and fifth town succumbed, we were no longer a coincidence. By then, the news began with square miles and refugees. On the day that the sizes included the names of three other states, there was barely room for a story about a deer in an untouched county with an arrow in its head, how, though surrounded by fence, it had been stalked. "How awful," the newscaster said, an enlarged photograph of the wounded deer behind him.

The Last

We have begun to think like snakes, aware of how we touch the smoldering earth. The copperheads have taught us, dragging our fear through the empty streets. Uneven, we've learned, this crust over fire. We watch our shoes for the first sign of collapse. The snakes swim on the soil. They surface through winter, disregarding the limits of their blood. Subsidence. Monoxide. Venom. Everything is feeding our choice. The snakes no longer think of ankles and feet. We coil. For now, what saves us are foundations.

THE PRE-NEED OBITUARY

This plan was foolproof.

Didn't the local newspaper, at deadline, take his mother's obituary on faith rather than fact-check, that much spot on? What sort of low-level editor in a hurry would confirm with a funeral home more than three hundred miles away, the one he'd Googled, careful to make sure he used a real name for one in her neighborhood? All he had to do after that was call in at work to leave a heartfelt message just before midnight. His car was already packed up with gear for camping and fly fishing. The three bereavement days he was allowed would run right into the weekend like a brief, but well-deserved vacation.

Yet there they were, three old women who hadn't yet moved farther south like his mother had, one after the other calling the newspaper first thing in the morning. As if they opened their newspapers at six a.m. As if they started with the death notices. Those crones were probably never even her friends, just Facebook addicts who saw his mother had posted only eight hours before, bragging about the weather. Busybodies who butted in, wanting to be the first to correct an error like it was some sort of community service.

He hadn't killed anybody. It wasn't as if he'd been stopped at an airport gate, his passport updated and ready to present for a flight to a country without an extradition agreement. He hadn't stolen anything but time. He'd slept in an extra hour like anyone would on vacation, so he wasn't even dressed when the police had arrived like characters in a parable for shame. Right away with the story of the three gossipy witches. Right away, their smirks. Right away with all of his fishing gear arranged in the back seat of his car.

Next, his immediate unemployment. Shortly thereafter, the story in that same local paper. A radio host using him as a punchline. The stares of his neighbors in his townhouse development. Look, he wanted to scream, "Didn't my mother say, when the newspaper called, she understood that her son just needed a little time to himself, no reason, at least, for him to be prosecuted?"

Now, all he wanted to say was there's another way of looking at this. He'd shown his mother nothing but kindness, his paragraphs listing her positives because he was a good son, proclaiming her decency while she still lived and breathed? He'd set the tone in the very first sentence, using the phrase "entered into heavenly rest." He'd launched, first paragraph, a boatload of her best qualities, cargo enough for sainthood, citing, first of all, her sixty years attending Lutheran churches exclusively no matter where she lived.

Hadn't his mother always preached, "Truth is in the details?" Well, he'd been specific and precise, showing even the skeptical how that early assumption had already taken place: Her years of volunteering with Habitat for Humanity and neighborhood recycling projects. Her late afternoons delivering for Meals on Wheels. Her belief in tithing.

What other mother could clip such passages and slip them in among her collection of cherished souvenirs? Whenever she felt like it, she could read about her perfection while she still lived and breathed. Best of all, she could show it to her new friends like a cherished photograph. Sure, there's a risk in that, but once they got over their smiles, she would enjoy, whether they showed it or not, the envy every last one of them would feel.

Angel Number

It had been so long since his father had died that Phelps had had time to develop heart problems of his own. At least his father could count himself lucky living to sixty-three with nothing but health until tumbling to the ground, still playing from the whites on the fourteenth tee at the municipal course. Phelps was fifty-one and thinking every flight of stairs was a bullet.

Two years ago, he'd had a heart attack in one of his classes at the community college. Business writing. They were learning the intricacies of the job application letter. They'd finished with the colon after the greeting, how this showed formality and respect and a sense of what the world expected from you if you wanted to work with your brain instead of your hands.

Just as he started in on the crucial first paragraph, how it introduced the employer to the applicant's qualifications and interest, Phelps had felt tightness in his chest and his voice had squeaked shut. Pain ran down his arm. "Oh Christ," he thought, "not here in front of the GED crowd and a bunch of mid-lifers," just before he was lost in the inability to do anything but sit and go helpless. "A warning," Phelps' doctor had said. "A wake-up call. A shot across the bow."

The doctor talked like that, in threes, like he believed in an angel number instead of science. "How are you? How you doing? Feeling ok?" Phelps wanted to answer, "Enough of that. Stop it. Shut up." Instead, he kept that triple play to himself like everything else, including his conviction that a mild attack was like a civil-defense-alarm minutes before the first nuclear missiles arced over the horizon.

Phelps had a son of his own who needed to listen up about his future. Twenty-seven years old. Maybe a decade before Drew would remember every chicken wing and cheeseburger as he climbed a flight of stairs. Like his grandfather, Drew believed not smoking and avoiding custard pie was the cornerstone of a healthy lifestyle while he grew heavy on pizza and cheese steaks and large strombolis with weekend, late-night binge streaming as if there was heroism in overeating.

His son worked night shift at the Hampton Inn. "It's good for me," Drew explained, describing how he read most of the time after he finished a midnight Mancini's delivery. Plus, he had access to the hotel's fitness room. He was building himself up with the free weights. "I go in at four a.m. when nobody ever comes in or goes out. I watch the news while I lift. It keeps me pumped, seeing how survival of the strongest is just around the corner."

"It's fittest, not strongest," Phelps said.

"They're synonyms, Dad," Drew said.

Drew sounded so much like his grandfather that Phelps shuddered when the weekend deliveries arrived from Mancini's three hours after Drew sat with him for dinner. Phelps' father, once, had said eating fettuccini alfredo was no different than riding a motorcycle. "What's the point of getting up in the morning if you worry so much?" he'd said. "You might as well wake up dead." Phelps had heard that expression a hundred times, but never outside of his family. It was like some characteristic passed down through generations, the shape of a nose, a talent for the sorts of puzzles that separated the quick-witted from the slow.

Wake up dead, he repeated to himself as he pushed a cart through the grocery store. It made him feel dizzy the way he did standing up quickly when he'd been drinking. He wanted to change the subject of his thoughts, but nothing came to him except the strange, distant voice of his father wheedling the chorus of that old "Eat, drink, and be merry" tune, its promise kept and filed in a mausoleum drawer.

In every aisle, there were packages filled with sugar and fat and salt. With cholesterol, carcinogenic dyes, and mysterious chemicals. A butcher stood alertly behind the extensive red meat display. The deli counter clerk sang along to the overhead speaker as she sliced salami.

It's better to have one big terror than a thousand small fears his father had said. The secret word had always been "consolidate," but Phelps had refused, until now, to say it aloud. For half an hour, he whispered it on repeat as he loaded his cart with colorful packages. They looked so much like presents that he opened one in the car, relishing the pleasure of each chip's salt and grease, its hint of lime.

I'm Doing the Talking

*Once, voters endorsed a policeman who
carried a ventriloquist dummy on the job.*

Hello, I'm special officer Anthony, here to sort out your domestic disturbance complaint.

Another policeman is always present, department policy, but I'm the one who decides what's equitable for both parties. Look at me when I'm talking. That policeman over there who's taking a drink of water can teach you something if you just listen. Before long, you'll recognize what you look and sound like to a man in uniform. Tell him to shut up and see who's doing the talking.

I mean it. Stop acting as if you don't want me to fix this. Take my word for it, he's the one who is thinking you two would be better off beaten for being a nuisance. Cuffed if you give anything but full respect. Get me? No? Try to imagine the possible outcomes of resistance. There's more where that came from, right? That policeman you're not paying attention to is itching to extrapolate.

You think I'm joking? You don't follow the news? Take my word for it, the voters approved me. Still have doubts? Don't you read the newspaper? Or watch tv? How did the both of you mark your ballots? You even recall the campaign? Who's your representative to Congress? What's the number of your legislative district?

Just as I thought. Now, listen up--my partner over there is sick of pretending he's here to ask questions. All those do is encourage lies. I'm the one a handful of your neighbors voted for—the truth that only hurts your soul. Look, he's put that bottle of water down, a sure sign he's tired of performing. Trust me, I don't have much more time to talk sense into you before your case gets adjudicated right here and right now.

Are you hearing me clearly? This isn't a house call. Adjudicated took me one hell of a long time to learn. Try that with your mouth full and see what happens, but first, the both of you, get down on your knees. No, don't ask what you've done to make me say that. Yes, like that for starters. Now drop and lay yourselves flat before he decides to dispense the justice he dreams about, the solutions he makes me listen to when he opens his mouth in private and speaks so distinctly that there's no talking back.

WRITING LETTERS FOR THE BLIND

Once a month, on Saturday afternoons, Craig wrote letters for Bill Nelson, who was blind from untreated glaucoma. Nelson's white cane always lay within arm's reach, but when he dictated his sentences, he gripped that cane and pulled his chair so close that Craig imagined him somehow reading over his shoulder.

Bill Nelson wrote to women he'd known as a high school student 600 miles west of where he lived now in North Carolina. Which was how he remembered them, never imagined going blind at forty. "She was a beauty," he said for each one. And nothing else. Nelson didn't have any photographs from his high school days. He didn't even own a yearbook, so Craig imagined what they looked like by using their names. Shelly was blonde and talkative. Virginia was dark-haired and quiet. Nancy had freckles. Beth was the prettiest of all but shy. Craig pictured them as he read aloud the letters that came in return, the lines scratched out in pencil or blue ball-point ink.

This is Craig writing, Nelson had him say at the beginning of each letter, and often, when those women, who were now about the same age as Craig's mother, wrote back, they added postscripts that began *for your eyes only* as if Craig would read their words aloud if they didn't remind him. *You're a dear*, Nancy repeated. *God bless you*. Virginia added. *We should all be lucky enough to know such a generous boy*. When Beth had her daughter write to Craig, she folded that page inside her letter so Bill Nelson, holding the envelope, smiled and said, "It's a good one, two pages."

"Just barely," Craig said, making up a paragraph to add before the *Yours in Affection* Beth had signed off with. He held both pages in his hand while he read what her daughter Melody had to say, how her mother wanted her to meet him, that the slope of his letters and his way of crossing *t's* showed he was a boy to be trusted in the fast-approaching 21st Century.

Only Shelly never wrote p.s. Her letters, after the first one, grew so short that Craig made up an anecdote to lengthen them, how she had left her husband and remarried. How she'd never had children. Had never even wanted them, but here she was living with a man who had five of them, but all full grown because he was eight years older than she was, a detail that made Nelson shake his head as if he was making up a story filled with better choices.

Nelson paid one dollar and fifty cents a letter, about three dollars an hour, half what Craig's sister made babysitting. Think of it as your gift, his mother had said. But soon, Nelson, stopping to tell old stories about the women as girls, went on for more than half an hour before he said, "Yours truly" and paused to pay Craig in nickels, dimes, and quarters from a fat change purse open on the table, measuring every coin by touch, always leaving it open like a test.

For months, Craig passed that exam, not stealing, but some nights, he woke and saw nothing as if his now-recurring dream had come true, the one where he made change in the dark, handling each coin in his black purse, unable to tell which ones were proper. The one where the number and size of those coins never satisfied someone he could not see.

At last, after six months, Beth included two one-dollar bills post-scripted for him. Bill Nelson touched each one, then let them lie quietly and thin on the table as Craig read, "The ten dollars are for your young friend," giving himself a raise.

Bill Nelson smiled in such a wistful way that Craig thought he was jealous rather than pleased. He wanted Bill Nelson to reconsider the size and heft of his coins, ask for a roll of half-dollars from the bank and hand them over like quarters. Craig waited, fixed on Bill Nelson's clouded, sightless eyes. He wouldn't steal from the blind, but he was ready to take what a good and thoughtful boy deserved.

QUAGMIRE

At the edge of our back yard, a soft bog formed. I was a sophomore, both old and young enough to test it with my shoes and half-expect hands upraised or a riot of worms. The neighbor's dog skittered away from there as if that quagmire smelled like death.

My father was worried. The swamp, he said, was spreading. Our house lay downhill, the slope just steep enough that some nights I expected thick slime to slip under the back door, bubbling and multiplying like the ancestry my uncle had traced, by then, all the way back to the 18th Century. "The begats," my father said, using the Bible-talk he loved. "He'll take us back to Adam if he has enough time."

In Biology, Mr. Freitag told us that Aristotle, the great thinker, had said inanimate things contained a "vital heat." The unborn waited in the soil, in dung, in cheese, in bread. The dew itself seethed with miracles, each morning giving birth to insects. As an example of spontaneous generation, what people believed for thousands of years, he read a recipe for mice: *Place sweaty underwear into a barrel and cover carefully with husks of wheat. Wait three weeks. Be patient. It takes time for sweat to penetrate those husks, but one morning, when you investigate, mice will emerge from that wheat, born from intimate perspiration.*

"Think about that," he said, meaning us to pay more attention to science, but I was thinking about the underwear, imagining what my lab partner, Becky Smarsh, might have next to her body. Two weeks earlier, Becky had dressed like a Roaring 20s teenager and flirted like a flapper in a thrift-store dress and a string of pearls at our class party. I'd worn my grandfather's silk vest and silver watch chain. Just before the party ended, I'd wrapped both arms around her, dancing like we were going steady.

During lab, we arranged our flasks like Louis Pasteur, openings straight up or s-curved, some covered, some sealed. We boiled broth and poured. We kept watch until that broth clouded and stunk or stayed clear, refuting the presence of what Aristotle had called "life-force" in air.

It was something to talk about with Becky after class. Laughing about Aristotle lasted all the way to the cafeteria where we separated to sit at different tables. Before lunch period ended, I made a stew of leftover cafeteria food, bits of bread and fruit, filling a condiment cup and sliding it into the hollow of a table leg. I ate above that brew for five days to see what might spontaneously generate. Most important, I wanted one more thing to laugh about with Becky.

On the fifth day, I bolted a sandwich and swilled milk before I raised that table while my small dessert stayed sealed. When I nudged that tiny womb into the light so I could observe the fine hair of mold and whatever else my recipe grew with time, darkness, and heat, a flurry of fruit flies lifted from that soggy cup as if I'd fathered them. They rose and dispersed, disappearing among three hundred third-shift-lunch-hour students before I stood, giddy, and hurried into the hall, carrying my cake as if I might offer it to Becky when I caught up with her for a minute or two of talking before we separated again for our segregated-by-gender health class.

Becky, a few months older than I was, had a brand-new

driver's license by the next week. She wasn't allowed to drive her father's car more than ten miles altogether at one time, but it was only three miles to the state game lands where teenagers parked in the large lot that was never used after dark. She found a spot near a distant corner and flicked the headlights on, then off, sending some sort of signal into the trees, creating, she said, the evening and the morning of the first day. "We're alone as Adam and Eve," she said, laughing as if the Bible was as silly as Aristotle. She flicked the lights again as she opened two buttons of her blouse. "For now," she said, "as far as I go," pressing my hands on her breasts in the dark.

"Yes," I said, so in love with just the partial knowledge of her body, that I was ready to say "yes" again and again to whatever she wanted to make fun of, even it sent us both to hell.

METAPHORS

When I was in kindergarten, my mother gave me a book that began with a boy in a striped shirt tugging at a stray string. Pretty soon he spins around faster and faster, the shirt disappearing page by page until it's gone. I'll be thirty-six this year, and I still have that book.

My mother and I loved that book. She called me Harry, the sweater boy's name, when she noticed a loose thread. One night, a few days after I'd scratched a thin line across my stomach while climbing a tree, she said, "It looks like you've been in a battle, Harry. You better stop picking at that scab or you'll unravel your skin and then where will you be, a soldier with all your insides unraveling?"

For days, I was terrified. "That was a metaphor," my mother said. "Get it?" but I didn't. I was afraid to touch that itchy scab. Or worse, pick at it. Underneath my skin were all the parts of me I never wanted to see. But before long, I lifted that scab with my fingernail and discover a thin, pink line that made me pull my shirt down to keep from staring.

"Light is pain," my mother said when I was fifteen and in love with metaphors.

"Sometimes," I said. "Bright light is a bully that loves to shine straight in my eyes."

My mother, thirty-six now, shook her head so slowly and slightly that I wasn't certain that she meant to disagree. "All the time," she said. "I mean ordinary light on a cloudy day. I mean what's outside no matter the weather." She waited, staring at me, until she seemed to decide I wasn't going to say another word. Then she told me her body was in a battle and losing.

"Who with?" I said. "How?"

"That's it. That's all you need to know about my little war story." She held out the damp, folded wash cloth she'd been squeezing as she talked. "Run some very hot water on this, would you? Wring it out and bring it straight back." I ran the faucet to what felt like scalding and squeezed the cloth, the water running hot under the cuffs of my shirt and down both arms. She laid it across her eyes and sighed. "This light is just a skirmish," she said.

I nodded, then caught myself and said, "Yes."

"Good," she said. "I knew you would. Your father shook his head. He made a face and mumbled, 'Say what you mean' when I'd already done just that."

"Like now," I said, though I was sure she would have given my father a straight answer – one with facts and details.

She didn't move the cloth. "Your father thinks he never uses them, but he doesn't tell his own war story straight. He keeps Iraq to himself like it's the combination to a safe. He thinks silence is just silence, but his is a fear of unraveling like little Harry. Remember?"

"Yes," I said.

She pressed the wash cloth down with both hands and took a breath. "The *Cliff's Notes* version would be 'Dying is more than a day job.'" She lifted the washcloth and looked at me. "Do they still have *Cliff's Notes* for students to cheat from?"

"I don't think so," I said.

She handed me the washcloth. "Do this again," she said. "Hot as you can stand it."

My father's war story was a faded, fringed shirt. My mother's war story lasted another four months before it ended. After that, it hung loose from me like a stray thread you might see on a sweater you're wearing, one you think will unravel the whole damn thing if you pull instead of snipping it off with scissors.

WHAT TROUBLE MEANT

The boy was a Tenderfoot, his father, the Scoutmaster who had been called to testify as a character witness for a young man on trial. The defendant, nineteen now, had also been a Boy Scout in his father's troop, and because his father had loved, when the boy was five or six, to take him along when the troop camped, the boy remembered that young man as a twelve-year-old struggling to make a fire without matches and losing a path marked by broken branches and a scattering of prearranged stones.

Leaving sleep for later, the boy's father had showered and changed after his bakery night shift, looking strange wearing a coat and tie and one of his two white shirts on a weekday. "A boy is in trouble," was all his mother said between customers while his sister waited with him, after Vacation Bible School, for a ride home when his father reappeared.

After his father returned from the courthouse, the boy was surprised that he stood in the bakery like a customer. That he waited in front of the display cases, speaking to his mother as if he was there to order a birthday cake for his daughter, maybe a girl just turning fourteen like the boy's sister. "I did what I could," he murmured and said he'd never speak of it again, life-sentencing himself to silence.

That night, the newspaper's front page displayed a picture of the man on trial. There seemed to be no question that the former Boy Scout had raped several teenaged girls at gunpoint in a county park. After his father left for work, the boy, still awake, crept down the hall. In the living room, using a flashlight, he looked up rape in the family dictionary. Now, he knew that trouble could mean something he'd never imagined, a secret he began to carry carefully toward his room. A few steps from his room, just outside her bedroom door, he could hear his mother, even this late, still talking on the phone. "It could have been worse," she was saying. "At least they were left able to tell."

His sister walked home alone from her 4-H meeting seven Fridays that summer, always on a busy front street. On the eighth Friday, the meetings ended, she carefully carried two dresses she'd sewn, eager, in August, to enter them in the county fair, girls' intermediate class, hundreds of handmade teen outfits competing for three shades of ribbons.

Those clothes were so clumsy in her arms, she said later, that she took a short cut along the narrow, diagonal street between two rows of tiny, flood plain houses where she was suddenly followed by a small pack of snarling dogs. One, at last, bit her as she crossed that neighborhood of the unleashed.

Soon after, the boy's mother told him to sit in the back seat and be quiet while she drove his sister to that neighborhood of dogs. The police rounded up owners and arranged their dogs in a growling lineup, but his sister was so hesitant when the choice was narrowed to two, that both dogs were loaded into a van while their owners cursed. "For rabies testing," the boy heard a policeman say, and even though he was safe in the car, the window barely cracked, the boy shuddered and began to cry while the rest of that pack of dogs barked as if they were marking his sister. As if, next time, they would show her what trouble meant and make sure she would never tell.

THE THEORY OF DOG SHIT

After I moved to Waverly during seventh grade, old man Krause was one of those guys my new best friend Charlie West and I hated. Because he came outside to curse at us when a foul ball from our makeshift field across the street rolled into his yard. Especially because he hid, once, behind his shrubbery and leapt out to pounce on a still-rolling soft-ball, refusing to return it.

The next afternoon, Charlie West explained the theory of dog shit, how a burning bag full would draw old man Krause to his front porch to stamp out the fire while we watched happily from a safely distant shadow. "Cool," I said. It seemed like such a great idea that the next weekend, I watched Charlie scoop a week's worth of his golden retriever's dog turds into a paper sack, then stood beside him in the April darkness while he lit the bag and rang old man Krause's bell.

Holding our breath because we were so close, we crouched on the street side of the same thick shrubbery Krause had used earlier in the week. But when Krause flung open the door, he didn't stomp on the fire. He just yelled, "I know what this is and I know who you are. I know your fathers, too."

Old man Krause didn't get his shoes covered in warm dog shit, but I smiled. He couldn't possibly know my father because my mother and I and my sister had moved to Waverly without him. Charlie grinned, too, because he knew that Steve Torok and Matt Kupchak were the two boys our age who lived on old man Krause's street, not a quarter mile away like he and I did, coming to that vacant lot just for softball.

They'd be surprised when the phone rang in their houses, old man Krause accusing them of minor crime. "They'll get grounded," Charlie said as we walked to our houses. "They'll be sitting in their rooms next Saturday while we burn more bags of shit."

And we did, testing the theory of dog shit on half a dozen enemy houses. Not once did a woman or a child answer the door. Only men, all of them someone we imagined we would hate just as much as old man Krause because their children bothered us somehow. Like the father of a boy who'd made fun of me when I'd moved to Waverly. Like the father of the boy who called us homos because we were always together. Like the father of a girl who, at the Valentine's Day semi-formal, told Charlie to "get lost" even before he asked her to dance. Like, at last, a house where we didn't know any-body because neither of us wanted to waste our last turd-filled bag and we were sure we'd hate at least one person who lived there.

But though half of the men cursed into the darkness, launching great obscenities of anger; and two walked to the edge of their lawns to peer into the darkness; and one frightened us into sprinting away by charging directly toward where we were hiding, not once did the man who answered the door step on the bag of shit. As if every man had already tested the theory of dog shit and found it flawed. As if that idea failed serious, prolonged examination. It was a myth, not science, not something any boy could replicate just by wish-ing it so.

TRANSLATING THE HAWK

Dependency kept doing its soft fly-by in what one couple finally called old age, admitting that each morning was broken into by a burglar who took nothing but more time. Their long-time neighbors gathered at mailboxes, sentries for medical chatter, but the couple walked the nearby river's shore each morning, counting the steps they believed extended their path to tomorrow. Though their lives had retreated into privacy, they saw others there who seemed to hold a similar faith. They nodded and lifted a tentative hand as conversation. They paused to watch the river's larger birds, blue herons and egrets, drawn to beauty even when the wife limped. Even when she used a cane. Even when she watched from the passenger seat of their slowly moving car.

Task by simple task, that couple paid others to maintain them while they endured the house arrest of embarrassment. Now, her walks were stutters from room to room. The husband, though he easily managed two flights of stairs, could not quiet his recurring panics, the latest so intense that he believed his body was vanishing, the nerves sputtering like doused embers going dark and cold.

His wife could not argue him to sense, her familiar reassurances unconvincing, her logic as insufficient as a walking aid. He had such determination to die of fright that she called 911, bringing the medics and the apparatus of rescue, but nothing could settle him except the reassurance of riding in an ambulance that used neither speed nor siren.

What patience everyone at the hospital had with his foolishness. Silently, he watched his vital signs testify to his cowardice. His wife endured the required four hours of observation without complaining aloud. Neither of them spoke as she drove him the twelve miles home.

The next morning, he noticed, as if for the first time, that each room was horribly tidy, the couch pillows exactly angled, the newspaper banished with the breakfast bowl and cup, the house poised as if expecting potential buyers. When the mail arrived, he did not retrieve it, certain the neighbors had eyewitnessed the leaving and returning of his tiny emergency. That they had considered the reasons for such short-term catch-and-release, pinpointing hysteria as the most likely trauma.

Late afternoon, she coaxed him to the deck for a late summer dinner despite August curling shut, brittle with heat. Mid-meal, she said, "Look. Do you see it?" and when he lifted his head, he saw a hawk perched on their roof's peak. At once, he thought that it could swoop down and reach them with its claws and beak before they could leave their chairs, but he kept still. For half an hour, it did not move, lifting only when they cleared their dishes, rattling the silverware.

The following morning, he rose before dawn to sit outside and waited as if the sky were television, a screen upon which the hawk would reappear. When his wife, worried about his absence, nudged the screen door open, he pressed one finger to his lips and she eased the door closed so softly that its latch-click was a whisper. The hawk, by then, was perched like a trophy.

For three days, because the hawk returned only in the early morning and late afternoon, they ate two meals on the deck.

Breakfast, prepared before sunrise, became elaborate and carefully prepared. Smoked salmon. A spinach and tomato omelet. Quiche Lorraine. And though neither of them could name the hawk's species, they were content with narrowing the choices by color and size, a male who they began to believe would keep returning as long as they were awake and eating.

The hawk on the house became a yoke of used time they gladly shouldered. They left their side door open all night because they wanted their emerging to be silent, just the screen's soft shuffle outward and back. For five days, the hawk perched exactly above them on the west end of the roof, a figurehead they began to translate the way they had learned to interpret the future, what it might be saying from another world which could only be reached through flight.

SURROGATES

A lot of seventh graders shoplifted. Sometimes I stood an aisle's length away and watched them slip stuff inside their jackets, but I never touched one item, not even the records I coveted. I couldn't get enough of them, but there was always somebody at school who wanted to show off, adding one of my favorites to the three or four they pilfered from the strip mall's discount store. Eddie Hoak even stole an album for me. "See," Hoak said, handing me the album as we walked down the sidewalk in front of the shopping center. "It's easy." On the cover, the guys in Devo were wearing yellow jump suits that made them look as if they worked at a nuclear power plant where they might be poisoned by radiation. Hoak was wearing a top coat like the one I wore to church over a hand-me-down suit. There weren't any other twelve-year-olds wearing top coats at the shopping center on a sunny Saturday afternoon in 1978.

A week later Steve Yates stole a cap gun for me. There was a time that spring when every boy in our junior high school wanted to make a zip gun, adding a barrel and a firing pin, attaching rubber bands to give more power to the hammer so it might be lethal. Or at least threatening. It was cool to talk about making a zip gun like that. As if I had even the remotest idea how to manage it.

Steve Yates came back from the K-Mart a block from our school with two cap guns while I was waiting for the late bus to take me home from band practice. They were smaller than the one my mother had thrown away when I was ten because, she said, "You're too old for this." I could palm one and then flash it like I was a real tough punk in Akron. I was wearing a hat tugged down over my forehead. It was black and had a little feather through the band, and I'd paid for it at the mall a month before. I punched Steve Yates on the shoulder and said "Cool," and I carried that gun around in my jacket for a week or so before I sold it to a sixth-grader for two dollars.

But for all that time when I wouldn't take anything from a store, I was stealing money from home. Quarters, dimes, nickels--nothing big, nothing I'd get caught for because how would my mother know whether forty-five cents was missing from her purse when it held more than four dollars-worth of change? I figured I could take 10% of the coins. It seemed like a safe number, something like church, what you're willing to sacrifice in order to protect yourself. My father just threw his in an old ashtray and never once missed how he was tithing to me every week.

I have a son that age now. Twelve. Just beginning seventh grade. I leave money lying around as if I am confident he will never touch it. Anyone would think I was as careless or trusting as my parents, but I keep track of how many dollars are lying loose on my dresser, how many quarters are by the phone in the kitchen. So far, Shawn has never taken one, but I think maybe it's because he's lived with his mother for the past two years and only stays with me every other weekend.

Or he recognizes my sting operation. Or because he wouldn't risk himself for chump change. Or because he doesn't have any friends in this town twenty miles from his school, nobody to have in the house on weekends who could be blamed for stealing change or even something larger. Something more valuable, convincing a boy who wants to be his friend to rob my house, drawing him a map to what can easily be sold, all my old 45's or my two manufactured guns or even my boxes of albums, things I keep but never use, things I wouldn't miss for weeks or months or ever but once upon a time was sure I had to have.

Zipper

As Wayne Strasser stepped back from the urinal, tugging his zipper up, he felt the head of it come off in his right hand. He looked down at his crotch. The zipper was up and closed, but even before he could say "Thank God," it began to splay open, and as soon as he moved, it split right down as if he wore the trick pants of a professional flasher, showing an expanse of white from his briefs.

Strasser stared at the piece of metal in his hand, and for a moment considered trying to work it back into place, seeing if he could get it started again, but he had less than a minute before he was expected back on line. He pulled his pants together and tightened his belt another notch, cursing himself for wearing tighty-whiteys instead of some dark-colored boxers more difficult to distinguish. Three and a half hours—maybe he could manage as long as nothing went wrong on the line to bring mechanics and the foreman, as long as nothing went haywire over on the next station, forcing him to help Ed Erdley lift a chipped head board or table top, something unwieldy that would surely spread his pants open.

Four hours later, undetected, he could joke about it when he told Louise, the woman he'd been living with for the past five months. He threw one leg to the side and his pants popped open. "Jesus, Wayne," she said. "You look like a man with special needs." He handed her the metal piece and pressed his legs together, but she was staring at the stretch of white that still showed, and he felt himself shrivel inside his briefs. "Take those pants off and let me have a look."

Strasser had them off in two seconds. He owned three more pair exactly like them for work, dark blue like everyone's on the floor. "Where do they make these anyway?" Louise said. "China or Hong Kong?"

"I think China and Hong Kong are the same place," Strasser said.

"That's two different names. They can't be the same place. And see here on the label. It's China all right. I knew it. I never saw an American zipper just come apart like this, not once ever."

"I mean Hong Kong's in China, you know, like New York's in the United States." Louise held the pants up as if she hadn't heard him. Spread wide, his pants looked obscene in her hands, like she was fantasizing something, and he was glad she didn't say another word about geography.

"You work in a union shop and they issue Chinese trousers," she said. "The slider was so cheap the pull jumped the tracks." Louise balled up the pants and dropped them in the wastebasket. "I think these are shot. I think that sweat shop where they were made ripped you and WoodWorld off, and that's all she wrote."

"Ok," he said, deciding to wait until later to retrieve the pants so he could turn them in and hope he didn't get docked for running them.

"Nobody saw you like that, did they?" she said, and for a moment, following her gaze, he nearly held his hands in front of his underwear.

"No," he said, but he was mulling over the words "slider" and "pull" as he walked into the bedroom, trying to decide whether the look she was giving him was the one she'd fixed upon her former husband a few times toward the end, one that was signaling he should rein in his long-term plans. He hurried into another pair of work pants, but before he went further, he slipped into the bathroom to relieve a pressure that surprised him with its urgency. After he flushed, he nudged the zipper up so carefully that he began to imagine a future in which every time he pissed, he would be cautious, looking down to make certain that the teeth were locked together in that perfect seam he'd always taken for granted. More than a hundred thousand times, maybe even a million by now, things had stayed perfect until today, just piss and pull and forget about it. Now, though, he ran one finger along the teeth before he washed his hands and walked slowly to the living room.

"Slider," he mouthed, touching himself. "Pull." Preschool words. Louise stared at his pants like an incredulous mother, disappointed that her son had grown up to be a fool.

AERATION

After his wife dies, her wine keeps arriving monthly, twelve bottles each from two clubs, the first his birthday gift to her, the second, more expensive, for an anniversary. To replace the first, he'd said, but she'd kept both. "Not that much," she would say when he began to count. "I share with my book club. A friend or two from time to time. I give some as presents." But now, without those reasons, the first two dozen, crated in the bedroom, seem to whimper for release. Soon, though each afternoon and evening is slow and endless, two dozen more arrive, and he has never cared for wine.

Though he never answers a promotion offer, the bottles, he knows, will keep arriving, selected by algorithms and automatically charged to their shared credit card. On her birthday, the complimentary prosecco from one of the clubs, from the other, her favorite, a *verdejo* from Spain. By the following month, when he finally unpacks all of the boxes, the bottles, mostly of dry whites, sprawl over so much of the bedroom carpet that he knows he needs to cancel.

She kept records of her passwords. The sites are bookmarked. But he hesitates, remembering that she once told him that well-stored wine will keep for years. He buys a dozen new wine racks. He arranges them in an arc in the bedroom that he has long-since abandoned, moving into the guest room after weeks of sleeplessness. All of those racks are bored so perfectly from oak that he stares into the circles before he slides the bottles in, so foolish with tools that it is impossible for him to name how tunnels were accomplished.

Soon, he waits to unpack, each month, until both clubs arrive. The days of anticipation seem shorter. The time spent unpacking is a blessing. But what he grows to love is watching the way the light plays on the twenty-four new bottles, the spectrum of colors produced by the variety of wines. Always, he lingers before storing them in the racks, opening the walk-in closet to her dresses, her skirts, her blouses, and the wonder of her rows of shoes. Always, he scans them as he relishes the idea that wine should be sipped and savored.

At last, after a year, he cancels. He lays the final order into the last open rack. All of the 290 bottles are horizontal. All are located in shadow, the room thermostat preserving a constant temperature, a dehumidifier keeping the humidity low, the door closed except for his entering and leaving. From among her clothes, he carries his favorites to the guest room closet. So much time has passed, the dresses seem new as he dreams her into the open and airy guest room. How her body was eager for his at intervals that always surprised him. How she directed him as if he were a naive bride.

Now, he begins to open the wine, carrying one six-ounce glass into the guest room each evening. Chardonnay. Sauvignon blanc. Pinot grigio. He imagines her declaring that each bottle, despite its age, is as pleasing as promised. Without fail, he allows the wine time to breathe. Glass by nightly glass, he finally sips and swallows, working counter-clockwise. He feels the future emptying itself, creating a space so wide and featureless that it seems like another planet, one with gravity that makes walking so difficult that he becomes breathless moving from room to room.

NEGLIGEES

Christine tugged their bedroom curtains closed by hand. "You can see right through these," she said. "They're like a negligee. Like whoever made them wants the woman in the bedroom to look sexy from outside. Like she's not even dressed standing there in the gauzy light."

"I don't think so," he said.

"All our neighbors shut their drapes as soon as it starts to get dark, but none of theirs are see-through."

"We're shadows. Lots of people have these. Our neighbors are like moles behind those thick drapes."

"We should leave them open so they see who we are instead of imagining," Christine said.

"They have better things to do."

"We should watch the Keller's over there across the street to see if they peek. They're our age plus a few years, and their boys are what, eleven and twelve? Those two are looking, you can bet on that." He stared at the closed, translucent curtains as if his wife had the Keller's and maybe some of their other neighbors figured out. For a moment, he considered going outside to see how Christine looked through the haze they created. Like the Keller boys, he thought, and laughed to himself.

"We used to walk outside in the dark," Christine said, moving into the kitchen as if she wanted him to follow her out the side door, the one they always used and asked their guests to use, leaving the front door to strangers.

"Years ago," he said. "The world's different now."

"I bet I could walk up and down our street in the dark and nobody would even know I was there. I could go out in slippers and a negligee of my own, a sheer one like these drapes."

"You'd be cold. You'd feel every piece of loose gravel right through those flimsy soles."

Christine gritted her teeth. "I bet I could walk naked and nobody would see me."

"What if they did?"

"They wouldn't recognize me." Christine said. He opened the refrigerator, then closed it, straightened, and said, "It's not that simple."

"That's what you think," Christine said, and stared so intensely at him that he felt she was reading his mind. "You look like a policeman. Like you're trying to figure how to get me to shut up without being scratched and bitten."

"This cop is going outside completely dressed," he said.

He walked the street up and back, wishing for a set of open drapes, but there weren't any. When he checked their house, he noticed that Christine had turned off the bedroom light, maybe even got into bed so she could pretend to be asleep when he returned.

He made a second circuit. Every one of the fourteen other houses seemed to be illuminated by the flickering light of televisions, but as he approached their house again, he saw that the bedroom light was back on. Christine was standing beside the bed and facing the walk-in closet.

From the street, through the thin curtains, his wife looked like a stranger, a woman whose body he had never seen. A silhouette. When she moved, turning to face him, she went so still that he was suddenly sure she was staring, imagining him another man. Trembling, he crept to the front door, rang the doorbell, and concentrated on nothing but remembering the silhouette before it had shifted and accused him. "Who's there?" a muffled voice said.

"Me," he said, and waited. It was all he could do not to turn around to see if the Keller's were watching. The door opened so slowly that it groaned. Ahead of him, the hall was unlit and empty. Without looking back, he stepped into the darkness and whatever would follow.

THE DEVIL'S CHILDREN

Your father's sins, Miss Sussex told us in September, belong to you, counting the ways from drunk to unfaithful while our Sunday school class constructed heaven and hell, silently attaching the future for all of us onto the church's new bulletin boards. Melanie Truman, whose father had disappeared, cut narrow spaces into heaven's gate, forming a grate so we could see inside where the white wings we drew floated against cloudless blue sky. Jack Walcyk shaped a purple robe for God and a loose, white cloak for Jesus, their faces turned away because we dared not look upon them. Remember, Miss Sussex said, those wings will only be lifted by the benevolent breath of God if you are pure in heart.

Children, Miss Sussex said in November, you are all just numbers. She read us Bible verses, speaking, she said, for a disgusted God. She assigned numbers for good and evil. Sunday school was 2, church was 4; lying was -3, stealing was -6; prayer was 3, swearing was -4. Always, evil subtracted more than goodness earned. The totals growled, teeth bared, when Miss Sussex made columns of figures she called hypotheticals. Children, she said, yes, all of you, your number can be zero, or worse yet, somewhere far below that where the damned are counted in minuses, and we thought about the negatives, saying nothing to each other, still believing, while we listened, that our secret sins were singular.

All winter, Jack Walcyk and I, near Pittsburgh, walked to fifth grade inside a coal-smoke cloud, passing the blocks-long Spang-Chalfant mill where the light and heat of molten steel poured over us like the weather would be, early morning, in hell. We made up stories of our own, one with a second sun drifting toward Earth, sweating children crying for water. At its end, we decided, cactus would rule, scorpions scuttling on a planet of sand until the suns collided.

Miss Sussex, by April, made all of us design the black wings for hell. Dick Wertz, his father in prison, scissored scarlet triangles for eternal flames. Melanie Truman cut a grate for the wide gate to hell that that Sharon Claus made, but Miss Sussex told Sharon to leave it open.

In May, Miss Sussex forecast weather for our hell, constant heavy rain. She had us cut gray clouds and sharp, silver drops that we scattered close to the clouds because every drop would vanish before it reached whoever was crying in the flames.

God sees into your sinful hearts, Miss Sussex said in August as she said goodbye on our last Sunday. Remember that, children--He knows every thought. Just you wait, there are sins you haven't imagined yet. Believe me, they can do more than add up—they can multiply.

The next Sunday we changed classes, boys and girls filing into separate rooms as we began to master the sins of lust and envy and coveting, using the sin of falsehood to deny how we privately abused ourselves and publicly blasphemed, counting the commandments we shattered each day even though Miss Sussex, each Sunday all that summer, had kept our paired, praying paper hands pinned underneath the dark red, detailed face of Satan she drew to remind us how he wanted to adopt us like stray puppies, training us to be the devil's children. We were divided now, growing into our fathers in one room or their victims in another.

POSTCARDS

My mother had a story she would tell when company came. Which wasn't often, and almost always on Saturdays. Another woman or two her age would sip drinks and eat Planter's salted peanuts my mother would pour from the can that she let me open with the key that was attached to the bottom. I loved doing that, inserting the soft metal tab into the skinny hole in the key and then going around, making sure to stay level because if I didn't everything would snag and she'd have to shake the salted nuts out through whatever size hole I'd made before the key got stuck.

The story was about my father, who worked night shift at the mill, and used to sleep during the day in the attic above our three rooms. We didn't exactly rent that attic, but nobody, and certainly not the landlord, ever went up there. One morning, he carried a cot and fan up the steps into the dust and heat. He said it was because he couldn't stand the pull-out bed, but what our mother said he meant was that though the kids had learned to be quiet, he felt that daylight-sleeping in the living room put him on display like a body in a coffin. The door was always locked, guaranteeing that was one more rule they couldn't disobey, going up there and one or both maybe tumbling out the low window to the alley forty feet below.

"Wally was a pip," my mother said every time, "and that last time he let the wanderlust get the best of him."

Word for word she said that sentence and the ones that followed until I could recite them myself, how my father had turned up in Alaska, sending each of us a postcard with the same message: "Hi there. I'm right here where you're looking." Each postcard was different from the others. Mine showed a grizzly bear in a forest. My sister's had a picture of a moose standing in a creek. There weren't any animals at all in my mother's card, just a lake with the sun going down behind distant trees. The women would nod and reach for more peanuts from the bowl that had a wreath of roses around its edge.

"And that was it," my mother would say. "It was like he went on a solo vacation and got lost in the wilderness. He didn't write one word about being sick. He had that cough with him the day he left like he always did. The sore throat he said was nothing to worry about, just because it had hung on for so long. My card said he missed me and wanted to get back to being a husband again."

If the women eating or drinking had never visited before, they would always look at my mother after "again" and smile as if her story might be working toward a happy ending full of "sorry" and "welcome home," and I would wonder, from the small bedroom my sister and I shared, what they were thinking, because anybody could see the story was pointed in another direction.

"Two weeks after those cards were postmarked," she'd say then. "To the day. Like he'd decided he knew how long he had and wanted to spare us the misery." She'd take a deep breath, and the women would reach for their glasses, giving her time. "That's it," she'd say. "That's all folks."

But she never mentioned her second postcard, the one postmarked four days after the others that included all of our names in the greeting. Not while I was listening at the door like I always did while my sister played with her dollhouse as if our mother wasn't out there talking to some stranger. For all I knew, maybe she was pretending she'd moved into a house with the Hulbertsons who'd lived downstairs with a daughter her age until a month ago.

Not that one with the picture of polar bears. Not what he wrote on the back about how he'd had his heart set on Alaska because it was the opposite of the mill. The space he filled in with letters so tiny our mother had to hold it up to the brightest lightbulb we owned to read. The message that end=ed, "It's only October, but it snowed. The kind that sticks and stays, not melting by noon like it does where you are, even in December. PS—Don't worry. I have a room with a beautiful king-size bed."

Christmas Sweater

An hour into his father's viewing, Hank Woolsey noticed his sister's husband Daniel walk in wearing a gray parka that he slipped off to reveal a red sweater circled by two rings of green and white prancing reindeer. "He was watching his football game," Jackie said, and Woolsey felt his fists clench. Daniel, after he shook Woolsey's hand, announced that Penn State already had a two-touchdown lead.

"It's just the end of the first quarter," he said, "so it still might get interesting."

"For whom?" Woolsey said.

Daniel looked perplexed. "You don't follow college football?" and Woolsey remembered how his father, though he loved watching football, had hated Daniel, how he'd worried that Daniel would outlive Jackie and squander all the money she saved by living frugally.

Fifteen minutes later, Jackie said, "Daniel thought you'd want to know nothing's changed." Woolsey turned away, but when he spotted the red sweater leaving the viewing room, he followed it. He watched Daniel disappear down a flight of stairs, and half way down himself, Woolsey could see into an office where there was a small television tuned to late October football.

Woolsey retreated, and when Daniel reappeared, announcing the half time score as if he'd placed a bet, Woolsey, to keep from cursing aloud, began to count the green and white reindeer that circled the sweater, losing his place when his brother-in-law turned. Starting over, he lost count again, their knitted hooves lifted as if prancing in snow.

After the next morning's funeral service, when he embraced his sister, she was so thin in his arms he thought she might be dying too. "You know how Daniel is about religion," she said. "Before you say anything, he's not here because he doesn't want to be a hypocrite." She stepped back and patted his right arm. "After the burial, come to our house for a nice lunch. Daniel's doing his part. He's hired a caterer."

By the time Woolsey and his wife Marilyn arrived, his sister's house was more crowded and less subdued than Woolsey welcomed. He picked at a small plate of cold cuts and desserts before asking Marilyn to say their goodbyes and going upstairs.

Twenty minutes later, Woolsey parked in his father's driveway. He opened the trunk and waved Marilyn forward. "Take a look," he said.

"In the shopping bag?"

He watched her until she looked inside, squealed, and swung around holding up the reindeer sweater. "You stole this stupid thing?" she said. "He'll know."

"He'll have to wear something else to Christmas parties. There's still two months. He'll think Jackie threw it away."

Nearly fifty years ago, his father had built a fireplace in his back yard and used it as a grill, keeping wood in the garage instead of charcoal, storing it next to his long unused golf clubs. Now, Woolsey gathered an armful and carried it to the fireplace. He built a tepee of logs and stuffed smaller sticks underneath it before soaking the whole thing with gasoline from the can by the ancient lawnmower. He didn't recognize the woman who was watching from her next-door porch, but he flapped the sweater like a flag and shouted "Hello."

He kept his thumb in place beside a hoof and began to count. There were ten reindeer in each of the three circles, the highest circle running just below the armpits. "I stole matches, too," he said.

"You'll blow yourself up," Marilyn said. "You'll be a ball of flame, and that stupid sweater will laugh if it has a mouth somewhere."

"I'm letting the fumes blow away. The can is back in the garage where it belongs. It'll just flare and then settle down to business." She stepped back as he struck a match, flicked it onto the pyramid and jumped away.

Woolsey hung the sweater along his father's four iron and dangled it over the flames. It flared in spots as if something highly flammable had been woven through the wool, the sort of material Woolsey imagined was used in clothes that immolated children. The old woman, he noticed, had gone inside, and he wondered if the police would respond to a call about intruders using a backyard fire place.

"We should get going," he said, stabbing at the remains of the sweater, a flurry of sparks erupting, each one of them so much a pin point of diminishment that he looked down again to make sure something that suggested a sweater's ashes was still there.

He scooped as much of what he believed to be the sweater's ashes into the shopping bag. Backtracked a mile to where the road to the cemetery crossed the highway. Six months ago, his father had taken ten minutes to locate his mother's grave. Hobbling, using a cane, he'd walked along the rows of plaques in the ground that lay lower on the shallow hill than the scattering of headstones.

Woolsey had been carrying daffodils, the mid-April ground

soft but not slippery under his father's hesitant steps. The sun had disappeared behind a set of thick clouds, the temperature plunging. "There she is" his father had said at last. "She's right here," and he'd handed the flowers to his father, allowing him to slowly bend and place them in the vase that was bolted into the plaque's edge.

Now, his father's grave fresh, the ceremony only hours earlier, Woolsey walked directly to the site, the shopping bag so light in his hand that he looked at it twice to be sure it wasn't open, the wind emptying it.

"Go ahead," Marilyn said, and handful by handful Woolsey scattered the sweater's ashes across the graves.

"So he knows," Woolsey said, and though he held no hope that this was true, he hugged his wife as if both of them believed it.

Headlights

Scott's new girlfriend punched his arm and called out Padiddle. He hadn't even noticed the car with one headlight, but he felt that punch. He was nineteen and hadn't played that game since he was twelve. It was immature and stupid, but Scott let it pass because he loved having that girl, a high school senior, press against his as he drove the family station wagon. With no car of his own, his choices felt narrowed.

Twilight drifted into full dark as he followed a familiar two-lane road. That girl, as if she could read his mind, said, "You know what? Padiddle is for kids. Ever turn off the headlights when it's dark?" She slid closer, her right hand resting on top of his where it gripped the steering wheel. "Try it," she said, breathing the words. Her breasts pressed against his side, and her breath in his ear made him keep his hands still. The road was empty and straight, exactly the conditions Scott hoped would last until she started to talk about something that didn't bring the sweat up out of his armpits and palms. She put her tongue in his ear, and he stared straight ahead, trying to memorize the highway's direction. "Go ahead. There's nobody coming." He switched the lights off and counted to five before pulling them back on. She sat back against the passenger door, and he thought, for a moment, that she was satisfied.

"This time, wait until there's a car coming our way. Let's see how it feels to be invisible in traffic." Scott checked the speedometer and saw it had slipped to fifty, her voice bringing him under the speed limit, something like his college grade point average plunging below acceptable. When a set of headlights came over the horizon, she rested her hand on his leg, her fingers kneading the inside of his thigh with so much pressure he nodded, watching the headlights until they looked about 200 yards away before he switched the lights off.

"Yes, like that," she said when, seconds later, Scott had the lights on again just before that car's horn blared past them. But even as her hand slid higher, he stayed soft. "You were afraid," she said. "You didn't get turned on at all." He thought about telling her it was fear of failure, not this stupid game, but she kept her hand on him as she whispered, "You know what would be really exciting? Driving in the oncoming lane without headlights as a car approached."

Mute, Scott concentrated on the highway. "I know what you need," she said as a set of distant headlights appeared. "You'll know when to save us." Scott could hear himself breathing as he reached for the light switch. "Do it," she said, and the road in front of them went dark as he veered into the oncoming lane.

"Yes," she squealed, her hand pressing on him as he stared at the oncoming lights, leaning forward.

"Scott?" she whispered, lifting her hand, but he hesitated until her silence saved them.

Years Later, the Once-Famous Mailed Girl Tells her Story

Not many children have been mailed, but, true story, I was posted like a crate of nails.

Listen, it's not that hard to imagine. Parcel post, that year, had a limit of fifty pounds, plenty of room for fitting a small child. Of course, I had to be weighed while the postmaster watched. My mother held her breath until the scale balanced at forty-eight and a half even with my shoes on.

After I was dressed to ship, my mother held me still as the stamps were stuck to my coat. "Only fifty-three cents," she said, her voice sounding the way it did when she brought me along to shop for bargains.

The boxcar clamped its jaws around me. Five years-old, arranged among the baggage, everything inside me seemed tightly gift-wrapped. Soon, I felt the folds in my heart set like wrinkles in laundry too long untended. Right then, I wished I was bagged, my shame travelling like a toothbrush, underwear, and a change of clothes.

At last, I remembered to breathe, nobody in that window-less, rolling house but me and the quiet clerk. Fear changed the large trunk I sat upon into a coffin, but I mastered the art of screaming to myself. Parcel post, I repeated for miles, trying to match the rhythm of anything I could hear until it slowed and stopped.

When I was handed down from the train, my lips were so tightly creased my grandfather ran one finger over them as if he was feeling for stitches. My grandmother murmured her breath upon my face to unlock me.

Take my word for it, I was the last, not the first child to be mailed. Go ahead. Look it up. There were babies posted in Ohio and Pennsylvania, both delivered safely, too. The weight limit, then, was twenty pounds. Understand now? When it was raised, my mother requested the price, comparing it to sending me as a passenger.

Like me, those babies have grown old, but they don't recall anything but what they've been told. I'm the only one who remembers being stamped to prove I belonged among the packages, the only one whose journey forced a law forbidding her mother's thrift.

Two men wrestled that trunk to the station platform, the weight of it bringing their breath to a boil of grunts. When my grandfather carried me past its bulk, I didn't say a word about imagining it a coffin because I was sure I could hear the terrified, muffled cry of someone large and smuggled.

LESSONS

In June, on Syd's thirteenth birthday, his mother looked at him, frowned, and said, "You're too old to drown. I signed you up for swimming lessons, a birthday present you'll thank me for more than once." The worst one ever, Syd thought, reaching for a second slice of cake. "Two weeks," she told him as he licked icing from his fingers. "The town pool is so close you can almost hear the splashing from our front yard." His father pushed his untouched cake aside.

The first day, ten middle-school boys, ages 11-13, jumped off the side of the pool to show they weren't afraid, and then, as if the lifeguard wanted to be sure, they held their heads underwater and counted to ten. They stood in the shallow end and made swimming motions with their arms. They did the dead-man's float. The second day, they held the side of the pool and kicked. They pushed a life preserver in front of themselves and kicked some more. "You're already ahead of your father," his mother said while his father silently formed and reformed designs made from his uneaten peas.

"First chance to test out is today," the lifeguard said at the end of their third lesson. "Some of you are looking good." Three boys ran to the deep end of the pool as Syd hesitated by the 4-foot sign. The lifeguard didn't say anything to them about running, but he looked at Syd and said, "You ready? You're big enough, for sure." None of those three boys looked older than ten. Syd outweighed the largest of them by thirty pounds. The lifeguard's logic seemed so sensible that Syd joined them at the 8-foot sign. "Down and back," the lifeguard said. "That's all it takes. Down and back and you're finished with beginners."

It started to rain while the smallest of those boys jumped in and treaded water like a duck. One by one, those boys aced that test and ran off through the downpour to wait for the lifeguard to sign their certification cards. "Ok, big guy," the lifeguard said, and Syd blinked the rain from his eyes and jumped, staying so close to the edge of the pool he nearly scraped his back open. For a few seconds, paralyzed, Syd held to the edge with one hand as if he needed to get reoriented. "Reach and pull, big fellow," the lifeguard said.

Syd extended one arm and started kicking, accelerating his feet as he felt himself sinking. He reached with his other arm as his face went under, thrashing like the victims in movies just as alligators or sharks dragged them under. "Reach and pull," he heard. "Reach and pull, goddammit," but he sank and barely kicked his way back to the surface. A moment later, he heard the slap of the life preserver as it hit the water beside him. "Swim or take it," Syd heard, and he draped one arm over it and let the lifeguard pull him in. "I don't get it," the lifeguard said. "You look normal."

Syd hung his tag back on the beginners' board and walked past those boys who were standing under an overhang clutching their tags. They looked at Syd as if they'd just learned he'd been held back for another year in seventh grade. His mother patted his hand at dinner. "You're growing up so fast," she said. Without a word, Syd's father left the table before they finished.

Instead of going to the pool the next day, Syd stopped at a bakery where he could buy two cookies for a quarter, then stood beside a news stand where he thumbed through magazines for free. He didn't go near the pool, but he soaked his trunks and dampened his towel before he hung them on a line in the basement. "You're so thoughtful," his mother said. His father didn't look up, pretending not to hear.

Syd avoided the pool until the last day when he looked through the fence and saw two tags left on the beginners' board. He didn't wait to see which boy was still trying to pass. He walked to the bakery and bought four raisin-filled cookies, and then, because the newsstand clerk cursed at him, Syd sat in a laundromat to eat them as if he was waiting for a load of wash to dry.

"Good," his mother said at dinner when he told her the lessons were over. "Somebody besides me needs to stay afloat here." His father's chair was empty because, she said, he wasn't hungry.

What Color Did

Color mattered. Sunday mornings, his father held out shirts and ties like a ring-bearer and waited for his mother to match them. While she was deciding, his father gathered socks and pants to show her. When early everything was selected, he held up the three sport coats he owned in brown and blue and what the boy's mother called olive-gray. Each Sunday, in those early days of the pastel shirt for men, his father had seemed too old for choice, but the simple era of the white shirt was gone for good. By then, so much depended on color, his mother's selections were medicinal, alleviating his father's shyness, uncertainty, and fear. Color therapy, his mother said, had existed since the birth of stained glass, those shades, especially blue, promising health if focused.

The boy had three blue shirts, but his allergies persisted. A thick sweater and his winter coat were blue, but he caught colds and strep throat. When he mentioned the failure of color therapy, she smiled and told him how, when she was very young, someone had claimed diseases were caused by the various shades of the body's elements falling out of balance. Then she laughed, showing the boy the advertisements that listed red for hydrogen, blue for oxygen, carbon's yellow, nitrogen's green. You too, the ad explained, can learn to properly shine colors on your skin above where your problems lie. "Color matters," she said, "but not like that."

His father faltered toward despair when, a few years later, patterns came to his shirts--pinstripes and plaids, madras and paisley and fields of flowers that made a perfect match seem impossible. Close enough, his mother began to say, holding those shirts and ties to the natural light. Close enough, yet his father turned tight-lipped in public, hearing doubt in that diagnosis. He seemed unbalanced each Sunday, welcoming Monday's early morning when he pulled on the full green of his uniform for work, cleaning up after children who wore their clothes like models.

Green was reassuring from seven-fifteen a.m. to four p.m. It gave his father confidence as he swept floors, emptied wastebaskets, and made certain to align desks and arrange chalk by their simple colors. On Saturdays, the boy's mother washed and ironed the two sets of green. She hung them with care, swallowed pills, lay down to rest, and one afternoon sent away for "The Healing Scarf" because its silk was dyed with so many colors it contained every shade needed for her recovery. She didn't laugh. She studied its guide to color's power. She didn't smile. She had already learned the precise location for her pain. For months, she wore the scarf over her bare skull to balance her brain's intricate rainbow, enhancing the shades of radiation and the felt colors of chemo because, she said, "Every little bit helps."

Then his mother died, her rainbow of clothes packed and donated. His father recalled only three combinations for "dressing up." He learned to wash and iron the plain shirts--blue, beige, and gray--laying them out with the ties and socks on the unused side of his bed. He repeated them through a year of Sundays, the six Wednesdays of Lent, Good Friday and Christmas and the irregular arrivals of funerals and weddings. More than twenty times a year then, the simple shades what he remembered about the best arrangement of color, dressing himself three ways for God, one for work, until the boy, a young man now, watched him become all silence, unbalanced, and dark.

HOLIDAYS

Every Friday night, beginning in November, you and your older sister Vanessa slept over at Grandma Ruth's while your mother took what she called her "holiday." At nine o'clock sharp, Aunt Sophia washed your hair in the kitchen sink because, she said, "It needs it." She told you to keep your eyes shut if you knew what was good for you. She pushed your head under the faucet for a hot rinse followed by a cold rinse, reminding you the whole time not to wriggle like you were still a baby in diapers.

At 9:30, you and Vanessa put your pajamas on downstairs where those three high-ceilinged rooms were the only ones heated by the coal furnace. You both stacked your clothes by the living room door, Vanessa on one side, you on the other. As soon as you and Vanessa climbed the stairs, you could see your breath. In Aunt Sophia's bedroom, the two of you tried to stay warm under a thick down comforter.

In the morning, you dressed in those clothes you'd worn to school the day before, handing your pajamas to Grandma Ruth, who put them in a shopping bag from the A&P to keep for next Friday. "See how much your mother loves you," Grandma Ruth would say every time your mother drove up during breakfast. "She's always here at eight on the dot."

You were eight-years-old that winter, Vanessa ten, and for months, on all of those Saturdays, your mother had laundry in three baskets on the back seat, sheets and towels and a week of clothes separated from light to dark for the Laundromat. You had hot dogs at the tiny shop next door after everything was dried and folded.

Your mother had two jobs because your father, according to Aunt Sophia, was "where the grass was green." She sat in the kitchen and drank coffee for an hour with Grandma Ruth while Aunt Sophia kept busy in the house, running the vacuum, dusting the furniture, shooing you ahead of her work if you weren't where you belonged, in a chair reading a book.

When it came time, she had you gather up the three waste baskets and dump all the paper and wrappers and tissues into one to throw into the furnace. After she opened the furnace's heavy iron door, she said, "Don't get too close and end up a pile of cinders like Wayne Ruckdaschel." While you waited with the empty basket, she shoveled coal inside, sometimes hauling buckets of ashes away, her thick arms straining.

Wayne Ruckdaschel had been a boy in your class until he'd burned up over Thanksgiving vacation. Aunt Sophia said he'd lit a candle in his room and fallen asleep. Nobody else had been home. "Who leaves their boy like that?" Aunt Sophia had said to your mother the day after the fire. "I bet they were out getting loaded, and they came home to the price they paid." She didn't say how anybody would know that.

In December, when you found a comb under a chair in your apartment, your mother said, "Where did that come from?" and threw it into a wastebasket. In January, when you discovered a pair of dark socks under your mother's bed, Vanessa said, "Put those back and shut up about it" when you showed her.

In February, after your birthday, Aunt Sophia didn't say a word about Wayne Ruckdaschel as she shoveled coal into the furnace. Instead, she said, "Before you know it, you'll be old enough to know what's what." She looked you up and down as if she expected you to tend the furnace next winter.

In March, your mother didn't arrive at eight. Grandma Ruth sipped coffee and watched the clock until nine. Aunt Sophia told you to sit still when you got up to gather the waste baskets. "It's still nice out," Grandma Ruth said. "You two go out and play in the yard."

Vanessa sat on the porch and watched the street. When it started to drizzle, you sat beside her. At ten o'clock, Aunt Sophia opened the door and said, "You two get inside before you catch your death out here."

Just after eleven, your mother came in carrying laundry in her arms. She walked right past you and everybody else and down the cellar stairs. When she reappeared, her hands were empty. She picked up the A&P bag and said, "Let's go," and you followed her outside.

"Darlene," Grandma Ruth called, her voice sounding so young you felt like you and Vanessa had vanished, but your mother didn't slow or look back, and you nearly ran to the car because the rain, by now, was falling harder and felt as cold as Aunt Sophia's second rinse.

FRIDAY WAS CONDORS AND WHOOPING CRANES

Fridays, Miss Spangler talked about the endangered and extinct. The girls cherished whooping cranes, whose numbers had fallen to sixteen. The boys loved condors, their numbers fewer than fifty and plunging.

Somebody, she said, knew where each of those condors lived. Someone checked on every egg. A zoo in Texas was trying in-captive breeding with a pair of whooping cranes. Everyone at the zoo was holding their breath because the world would be less without whooping cranes. "You will be less, too," she said, "like only children." No one said anything. One by one, we looked at the four classmates we knew had no brothers or sisters, their parents, according to our mothers, selfish or sadly incapable.

"Think of the birds like this," Miss Spangler said. "There are twice as many of you than there are of those beautiful cranes. Soon, there will be more of you than condors." She paused and looked from row to row, the signal for *This is important*. "That includes everywhere in the entire world," she very slowly said. "Think of them as yourself. Think of searching for someone that looks like you and never seeing another child's face."

We whispered to each other. We knew where everybody lived, even the boys and girls who lived at RFD with a #, their mailboxes bunched at the end of roads that rutted and still threw up dust in 1956. The rest of us had moved to where some farms had been covered with tiny villages called Best-

View and GlenView, the streets named Magnolia, Cherry=
wood, Dogwood, and Spruce. Miss Spangler frowned.

Next Friday, Miss Spangler showed us a picture of a dodo.
"Not a real one," she said, "a replica reconstructed from bones
and feathers because they were already gone forever. They had
no predators where they lived. They were large and flightless
and such easy targets they were thought stupid for not try=
ing to hide."

"Dodo," two boys said, pointing at each other, and the class
laughed, even the girls.

Miss Spangler hissed. "Listen," she said. "Once, there were
so many passenger pigeons that they formed dark clouds.
Tens of millions, far more than the number of people who
lived in this country. More than the number who live here
now. None of them were flightless. Nobody believed they
could disappear, and now there are none."

Nobody called out "passenger pigeon." Miss Spangler
walked up and down the aisles and told us to imagine our=
selves being talked about in less than a hundred years. "I mean
humans," she said, "the species. When everyone is gone. Your
children. Their children. When all the views have no people."

The class was quiet. Everyone crouched as Miss Spangler
swept past their desks. "Those views are called landscapes for
a reason," Miss Spangler said. "Are you listening now? Here
are some ways a future without us could happen." By the
second reason, the girls began to sob. By the third, the boys
shuddered as they tried not to cry.

Acknowledgments

Albatross	*Fractured Lit*
The History of the Baker's Dozen	*Ilanot Review*
Extant	*Pithead Chapel*
Beauty	*Ilanot Review*
Teaching English in the Biology Lab	*100 Word Story*
The Plagues in Order	*Wigleaf*
After the Death of Sons	*Bending Genres*
Where Boys Waited for his Daughter	*Flash Boulevard*
Standing around the Hearts	*Bending Genres*
Elevations	*Atticus Review*
How My Mother Posed Me	*100 Word Story*
Tapeworm: A Parable	*South Florida Poetry Review*
Marking the Solstice	*Atlas and Alice/10x10*
Sideshow	
Tractors	*New World Writing*
After Hospice, the Uses for Liquor	*jmww*
The Hands	*Flash Boulevard*
During the Plague Years	
Inflatables	*Ghost Parachute*
Little Pricks	*Ghost Parachute*
Shadowing the Gravedigger	*Flash Frog*
Shopping for the Future	*Fictive Dream*
The Bedroom Clowns	
I Married a Monster from Outer Space	*Flash Boulevard*
The Drive-Thru Peep Show	*Fictive Dream*
Ash Wednesday	*Centaur*
The Year of Spooling Backward	*Pithead Chapel*
The Bottled Ghosts	*Vestal Review*
Prom Weekend	*Ghost Parachute*
After January's Active Shooter Drill	*Flash Boulevard*
The Guest-Closet Ball	*Flash Boulevard*
While he Still Drives his Father's Car	*Flash Boulevard*
Happy Endings	*Ghost Parachute*
Hansel	*Flash Boulevard*
Boxing the Future	
The Times	
Stunned	*100 Word Story*
Wail	*New World Writing*

Summiting   *Flash Boulevard*
The Look-Alike Doll   *Dribble Drabble Review*
IQ Test   *Moon City Review*
Kafkaesque
The Au Pair   *Cult/ Talking River Review*
The Year of Extravagant Additions   *Ghost Parachute*
After Six Years, the News   *Shorts*
Lazarus in the Forest   *Flash Boulevard*
Among the Swings
Apocalypse   *Ghost Parachute*
The Pre-Need Obituary   *Fictive Dream*
Angel Number
I'm Doing the Talking   *Flash Boulevard*
Writing Letters for the Blind   *Maryland Literary Review*
Quagmire   *Fictive Dream*
Metaphors   *Pithead Chapel*
What Trouble Meant
The Theory of Dog Shit   *SoFloPoJo*
Translating the Hawk   *Shorts*
Surrogates   *Best Flash Fiction*
Zipper
Aeration   *Ellipsis Zine*
Negligees   *Flash Boulevard*
The Devil's Children   *Fictive Dream*
Postcards   *Fictive Dream*
Christmas Sweater   *Gargoyle*
Headlights   *Ghost Parachute*
Years Later, the Once-Famous Mailed Girl Tells her Story *Flash Boulevard*
Lessons   *Fictive Dream*
What Color Did   *Monkey Bicycle*
Holidays   *Fictive Dream*
Friday was Condors and Whooping Cranes

Sections of Boxing the Future were published by *Atticus Review,
Flash Boulevard, Tiny Molecules, Cult, 10 X 10, Vestal Review, Lake
Effect, Pithead Chapel*
Sections of The Times were published by *Ghost Parachute, Atticus
Review, Pithead Chapel, Brilliant Flash Fiction*

ABOUT GARY FINCKE

Since its inception, Gary Fincke has been co-editor (with Meg Pokrass) of the annual anthology *Best Microfiction*. His books have won the Flannery O'Connor Prize for Short Fiction, The Robert C. Jones Prize for Short Nonfiction Prose, and what is now the Wheeler Prize for Poetry. His latest book is a memoir-in-essays *The Mayan Syndrome* (Madhat Press, 2023). Besides having work chosen to appear in *Best American Essays 2020* and *Best Small Fictions 2020*, he has recently published flash fiction at such sites as *Craft, Wigleaf, Vestal Review, Atticus Review, Ghost Parachute, Pithead Chapel, New World Writing,* and *Flash Boulevard.*

112 Harvard Ave #65
Claremont, CA 91711 USA

pelekinesis@gmail.com
www.pelekinesis.com

Pelekinesis titles are available through Ingram, Gardners, directly from the publisher's website, and at your favorite local bookstore.